THE CLOVER CLUB
AND THE HOUSE OF MYSTERY

THE CLOVER CLUB
AND THE HOUSE OF MYSTERY

A. D. LANGHOLM

A TARGET BOOK

published by

the Paperback Division of

W. H. ALLEN & Co. Ltd

A Target Book

Published in 1978
by the Paperback Division of W. H. Allen & Co. Ltd
A Howard & Wyndham Company
44 Hill Street, London W1X 8LB

Copyright © 1978 by A. D. Langholm

Printed in Great Britain by
Richard Clay (The Chaucer Press) Ltd, Bungay, Suffolk

ISBN 0 426 20053 5

Contents

The House of Mystery

'You must be joking, Sarah,' said Gillian. She sounded quite scandalised. 'Me? Come with you while you poke round that creepy old place? I can think of better things to do.'

'Oh, Gillian, it's not as creepy as all that.' Sarah Brownbridge was trying to keep her voice low because her father was in the next room putting up a new curtain rail. Although he always told her she was quite free to use the 'phone he sometimes got niggly if he overheard her talking for any longer than about sixty seconds.

'What? Not creepy? And there's that old woman living there. The hermit. What did Kate's father call her – the batty old lady of Lockets?'

'That's just some silly story, I expect. Gillian, you know I'm dying to look at the place again and compare it with the photographs and –'

'I don't know why you find those pictures so fascinating,' said Gillian. 'Anyway, if you don't think the place is creepy, why nag me to go with you? Off you go by yourself.'

Sarah sighed.

'Don't you have any sense of – of adventure?' she asked.

'Don't be soft,' said Gillian.

Sarah sighed again.

'See you at school tomorrow,' she said.

'Last day of term, isn't it,' said Gillian. 'That's something to look forward to, anyway.'

As Sarah put the 'phone down she was wondering if it was worth trying anyone else. Kate Freeman, perhaps. Or Corinne Ainsworth.

'But what's the point?' she thought. 'They'd think I'm

being stupid, just like Gillian does.'

She liked Gillian. She was her best friend at school. But there were some things she didn't understand. The photographs, for a start ...

In months to come, Sarah was to look back and reflect that it was perhaps as well that Gillian hadn't understood. If she had, everything might have turned out very differently. It's likely that Sarah would never have become involved with that strange old house by the river in the way she did. And that she would never have been invited to become the fourth member of that exclusive and adventure-loving band, the Clover Club. She would have missed such a lot ...

But, of course, she didn't know that then.

Sarah went upstairs to her room and looked at the photographs again.

She'd always liked old photographs and picture postcards and she'd collected quite a few of them. But these were something special.

'There's something about them that makes little shivers run up and down my spine,' she thought. 'Nice shivers, though.'

She'd found them at one of the antique-and-junk stalls in Cherringham Saturday morning market. They'd been inside a brown envelope which itself was inside a cardboard box containing a large number of other photographs, most of them fairly modern. Perhaps they were clearings-out from some bankrupt commercial photographer's store-room.

The pictures were brown and slightly faded, giving Sarah the impression that she was having to peer back into a misty past. They had been taken at what appeared to have been a garden party held long ago at a large riverside house. It had been a warm summer's day and the photographer had turned his camera this way and that, capturing groups of people on the lawns, and punters out on the river.

Scenes of beauty, gaiety and luxury. A lovely, romantic house. Lawns sweeping down to a river overhung by willows and lined by boathouses and a landing-stage. Sarah

8

had thought the period might be Edwardian, judging by the fashions.

She had been instantly riveted. The camera had frozen a golden afternoon of long ago and transported it to her as she stood in the market place in the drizzle. She had an ache to be at that garden party.

The funny thing was that she had felt she'd seen that house before.

One of the pictures had moved her even more than the others. It was of a girl, perhaps about seventeen years old. She was very beautiful, with an elfin face, and wearing a flowing, ankle-length, belted dress. She was poised in front of a fountain as if she had been running and had just come to a sudden halt, her eyes fixed forever on something unseen beyond the camera. Whatever it was, it seemed to bring her intense joy.

Sarah had stared at that picture for a long time.

And then she had happened to turn over the envelope. On the back of it, in beautiful handwriting, was written the words:

July, 1914. Garden party at Lockets.

Lockets!

So that was why the place had seemed familiar! She *had* seen it before. It all came back to her.

It was the time she and Gillian and Kate Freeman had gone out in a boat with Kate's father. They had explored far up the river, rowing along through mysterious winding tunnels of green foliage until suddenly it had opened out and there, set way back from the bank in its huge grounds, had been that strange house. It had looked deserted, a decaying mansion set in a rank jungle of overgrown lawns, a broken landing stage, rotting boathouses. Kate's father had told them that some recluse was supposed to live there, some batty old lady.

Lockets!

They had turned back at that point but Sarah had watched the house till it was out of sight, wondering about that old lady. She had fancied she saw a wisp of smoke

9

coming from the chimney but it might have been imagination.

And here was Lockets coming to life again in some pictures found on a market stall. Those scenes of luxury and gaiety had taken place on those same overgrown lawns.

What, Sarah couldn't help wondering, had happened in the years between?

She had paid ten pence for each of the pictures and taken them away. And ever since then she had been thinking about getting her bike out and finding Lockets. She knew it couldn't be more than three or four miles away from Cherringham by road.

She wanted to have another look at that mysterious house, compare it with the pictures, imagine the garden party taking place on the lawns again. The thought intrigued her.

'But Gillian *is* right,' she admitted to herself, ruefully. 'The place is a bit creepy. I don't particularly want to go on my own.'

It was now Thursday evening and it had been raining steadily all week so there had been a good reason for not going. But now the sun had come out and it had developed into a golden July evening.

'Anyway, I *am* being stupid,' she thought. 'They're just some old photographs.'

She put them back in the envelope and went downstairs.

'Did I hear you on the 'phone a minute ago?' said her father.

He was still wrestling with the curtain rod. He seemed to be making a mess of the job and was becoming exasperated as a result. It was probably making him think of his 'phone bills.

'I was just 'phoning Gillian, Dad,' said Sarah, and went out into the garden before he could start dropping hints.

Her mother was out there, gossiping to Mrs Winfield next door, as she had been for the last half hour. There was something about the evening sunlight falling on Ashley Crescent that made Sarah feel wistful, even sad. For some reason it brought the pictures back into her mind even more strongly.

She suddenly made up her mind.

'Mum,' she called. 'All right if I go out on my bike? I'll be a little while.'

'Yes, Sarah. Lovely evening for a ride. Watch out for traffic.'

'Yes, Mum.'

'And make sure your lights are working if you're going any distance.'

'Yes, Mum.'

She was going there: by herself: without any further thought.

Sarah went back up to her room and put on her denim jacket over her cheese-cloth blouse and flared blue jeans. Into the pockets she put the pictures, and carried her torch – just in case – and her father's ordnance survey map of the area she found in the landing bookcase.

She was suddenly feeling quite daring and excited.

'It seems like a little adventure once you stop talking to glooms like Gillian,' she thought. 'I suppose she's stuck in front of her television by now.'

Her father was trying again with the curtain rod as she passed through the sitting room. He seemed to be having difficulty boring the holes in the right places.

Her mother and Mrs Winfield were still gossiping.

'Sarah's a bit of a loner, isn't she,' said Mrs Winfield, watching her cycle off, brown hair flopping as she pushed against the pedals.

'Oh, she's got plenty of friends,' said her mother. 'But she's a bit dreamy. She's always telling me I don't understand her.'

She laughed.

'I don't.'

In appearance, Sarah wasn't especially pretty. She knew that, and was sometimes a little sorry about it. But she had a pleasant, blue-eyed, dreamy face. Although she was reserved, even shy, with new people, she was very animated

11

once she had got to know someone.

Her home was on the edge of the small riverside town of Cherringham and as she cycled out along the main road she could see across the fields red and white sails. The sunshine had brought them out like magic.

Lockets stood beside a little-used branch of the main river and after about half a mile she turned left towards it, following the map.

She was on a narrow, secretive little road that wound through dense woods. She knew that after two or three miles the road would divide, the right hand fork leading her straight to Lockets.

The hedgerows were at their lushest, dense with scents and little sounds of summer, rustles and twitterings and croaks. Sarah reflected that nothing around here could have changed very much since 1914.

But when at last she came to the fork she stopped, disconcerted, putting one foot on the ground.

It was just as she had known it would be from the map. The proper road swung round to the left while the little road to Lockets continued straight ahead.

It was a narrow road, rutted and pot-holed, crowded in by dense, dark trees amongst which it disappeared. By the side of it was the cause of Sarah's hesitation, a large sign saying firmly PRIVATE ROAD. It was old and stained and leaning, but it was enough to deter her.

'Maybe I can just scout around a bit,' she thought.

To her right were woods. A few minutes' walk through them would bring her to the branch of the river along which they had rowed and the footpath which, according to the map, ran alongside it. By turning left and following the river she would come to the house without having to venture along the private road.

She parked her bike among some bushes and entered the woods.

It was very still in there, the ground carpeted with ferns and moss, rays of sunshine glinting down into the clearings. Probably it had been planted as a pleasure ground in Victorian times for there had once been footpaths and rides for horses, though now they were overgrown with great masses of bramble and thorn. The clumps got thicker as Sarah approached the river and she had to make detours to skirt them.

'It's becoming quite a struggle to get there,' she thought, having scratched her wrist while parting some brambles. But it wouldn't have occurred to her to turn back now. She just wished she had someone with her, someone who would be as intrigued by the pictures and by Lockets as she was herself. Someone who would understand their fascination.

But there probably wasn't any such person.

From somewhere ahead she thought she heard a faint whistle.

She glanced up but instantly decided that if she had heard anything it must be a bird. She would be very unlikely to meet anybody in these lonely, silent woods.

But it hadn't been a bird.

Sitting high in the fork of a tree, some distance ahead of her, was a boy of about Sarah's age, a round-faced, cheerful boy, not very tall but wide and strong-looking. Until the sudden appearance of Sarah he had been sitting comfortably, hands clasped behind his head, humming to himself, but the sight of her walking straight towards his tree had galvanised him into action.

At his whistle, two other boys appeared below, their perspiring, inquiring faces upturned towards him. By the look of them, they had been working very hard.

'Girl coming,' he hesitated. 'Heading straight for us.'

'Are you sure, Rodge?' said one of the other boys.

''Course I'm sure, Tom. She's nearly here — scared she's going to see me now.'

Tom recovered his composure. He was a good-looking boy and the others looked at him expectantly as if he were the leader.

'Right,' he said, turning away quickly. 'Shin down from there and keep her talking till we've got the equipment out of sight.'

To the third boy he said:

'Come on, Graham, quick. It won't take a sec.'

Graham was dark-haired, lean and angular with an expression that was normally rather morose, though it could be lit by sudden, vivid smiles. He wasn't smiling now.

'The Skipper did warn us, didn't he,' he said.

Rodge came down the tree as if it were a greasy pole. He was leaning against it idly when Sarah, unaware of the consternation she had caused, rounded a great clump of brambles and saw him.

'Hi,' he said. 'Where are you going?'

The words were a little aggressive but the smile was friendly.

Sarah had made her first contact with the Clover Club.

2

A Vision from the Past

The sight of Rodge made Sarah jump and she halted. Then she realised that his face was familiar. She'd seen him some-times around Cherringham, one of a group of three boys who seemed inseparable. There was him, and a fair-haired boy . . . and a darker one . . .

Anyway, he wasn't anything to be afraid of.

'That's my business,' she said, and moved to pass him.

Instantly he stepped in front of her. 'I was just wonder-ing where you were going,' he said. 'Funny place to be all by yourself.'

'I'll go where I want,' said Sarah indignantly.

But he continued to stand there, and Sarah wasn't sure what would have happened next if the other two boys hadn't suddenly appeared behind him.

'Rodge making a nuisance of himself?' said the leader of them. 'If there's one thing that Rodge is good at, that's it.'

It was the fair-haired boy. He was smiling at her and Sarah's indignation faded. Rodge moved aside looking a little sheepish.

'Just curious,' he said.

Sarah walked on, puzzled. It hadn't escaped her that although the two boys had sauntered up casually they were grimy and dishevelled as though they had been working very hard.

'That was all a pantomime for my benefit,' she thought. 'They were hiding something. Can't imagine what, though.'

She noticed that somebody, possibly the boys, had been cutting away some of the brambles and thorns that choked the trees. Path-clearing, perhaps? But that was hardly any-thing to be secretive about.

'Oh well,' she thought, 'I don't suppose I'll ever know. It

won't be anything very important, anyway.'

She realised she was a little envious of the boys. It was because they seemed so inseparable. The fair-haired one had a nice smile, too. She should have returned it.

Tom was leaning against a tree, having a rest.

'That was a bit heavy-handed, Rodge,' he said, reproachfully. 'You might just as well have shouted into her ear that we've got something to hide.'

Rodge was squatting on his heels, back against another tree.

'I know,' he said, shifting uneasily. 'She caught me off my guard. I didn't really expect anyone to come this way so I hadn't thought what to say.'

'We'll have to be better prepared in future, won't we, Graham?' said Tom.

Hands thrust in pockets, Graham was still staring gloomily in the direction taken by Sarah.

'Hope it's not too late for that,' he said. 'Why's she wandering about these woods by herself?'

He looked round at the other two.

'The Skipper *said* we'd got to take care to keep it secret. I just hope we haven't been rumbled already.'

A few minutes later, after ducking and dodging her way along the overgrown river path, Sarah arrived at the brick wall that surrounded the grounds of Lockets. It towered high and smooth and ended in a great buttress that rose out of the river bank. There wasn't any hope of seeing over it.

Set in the wall was an archway with a wrought-iron gate through which the footpath had once continued. Sarah pressed her face against the bars of the gate, but she could see very little because of the bushes growing just inside.

Frustrated, she stepped back and looked about her. She hadn't come all this way to turn back without getting a good view of the house.

By the buttress an old, cracked, gnarled willow tree leaned out over the river. It rose higher than the wall and Sarah saw that where the branches left the main trunk they formed an enclosed little platform from which the house and grounds would be visible. It was quite an easy climb and she scrambled up.

It was comfortable up there. Sarah was able to seat herself almost as if she were in an armchair, her back against a branch.

The grounds of Lockets were spread in front of her, rank, sweet-smelling and forlorn. Nearest her were the lawns, invaded by dandelions and thistles, studded with great trees and criss-crossed by formal paths. Beyond lay the shrubberies and rose gardens.

And there, lifeless now, the water long since having ceased to play, was the fountain by which that girl had stood.

Sarah took the pictures from her pocket and put them on her knee.

Instantly the grounds of Lockets leapt to life again in her imagination. The garden party was taking place and people were moving about on the close-cut lawns. The fountain was playing, making hazy rainbows in the sunshine. On the river, the young men were laughing and calling to each other from their punts; the young ladies were trailing their hands in the water, their broad-brimmed hats tilted over their eyes to protect them from the sun as they gracefully reclined.

But no. They'd all gone, long ago. All that was left now was decay, lengthening shadows, a mist starting to rise from the water. And, for Sarah, a peculiar sense of loss.

'But they were there,' she thought, 'and in a way they still are, frozen by these pictures. Like shadows, or ghosts.'

She looked again at the picture of the girl.

'And that's the exact spot where she was standing by the fountain . . .'

Sarah's gaze travelled the lawns; to the rotting, tumbledown boathouses and landing-stage.

'The girl was looking towards the landing-stage. It was something happening there that was making her so happy.'

'But who was the girl, I wonder?'

Sarah's gaze travelled all the way back up the lawns again and came to rest on the house itself. It looked secretive, mysterious, withdrawn. It was hard to imagine that anyone was living there and yet as she peered at it, Sarah saw that there was again a wisp of smoke at the chimney.

'Is she the person who's still living there now? Could that lovely, elfin-faced girl be the batty old lady of Lockets?'

Amazing, impossible thought!

Yet who *was* the old lady who lived in Lockets? What was her history? Why was she living in that great house all alone?

Her interest stirred by the pictures, Sarah had tried to make some inquiries about her locally. Not many people knew of her existence and those who did had mostly heard only vague rumours. Only from Mr Barron, the baker's delivery man, had she got any solid information. It appeared he delivered a small loaf there three times a week.

'What's she like then?' Sarah had asked him. She'd been getting some cakes for her mother and, seeing him loading the van at the back of the shop, it had occurred to her that he might deliver at Lockets. She'd struck lucky.

'I've never seen her.' Mr Barron was a rosy-faced, chuckling sort of man. 'I leave the order in the cupboard by the side door and once a month I find a cheque there. I expect the other roundsmen do the same.'

'But if you've never seen her, how did you know to call in the first place? Did she 'phone?'

'That place isn't on the telephone. Not even on electricity. No, I expect we've been delivering there since the year dot.'

'And what's her name? How does she sign the cheques?'

'Maybury. C. A. Maybury.'

'But ... an old lady living alone like that! Shouldn't somebody be looking after her?'

'Nobody can go poking their noses in if they're not invited.' Mr Barron had chuckled. 'And she doesn't exactly invite anybody.'

There was a slight chill in the air now and Sarah was getting stiff.

'Anyway, what's it matter?' she thought. She put the

pictures back in her pocket. 'It's all nothing to do with you, Sarah Brownbridge. You've satisfied your curiosity so you may as well go now and get home before dark.'

But she didn't stir. Even when the light faded and the moon came out she still continued to sit in the willow tree. She was telling herself that despite the chill and the stiffness it was pleasant sitting there listening to the lap of the water below her, promising herself that after just a few more minutes she would go.

But in her heart she knew that she was waiting for something and that she wouldn't go before it happened.

It was dark and it still hadn't happened.

'You idiot,' she told herself fiercely. 'Why don't you *go*? They'll be wondering where you've got to at home –'

And then it *did* happen. In one of the ground floor windows of the house a faint light appeared. It gradually grew stronger, then remained steady, but it was still a dim, soft light.

'Gaslight,' murmured Sarah, wide-eyed. 'There isn't any electricity at Lockets, of course!'

So that proved it. There really was someone living there.

'I suppose that up till now I haven't really been able to believe that Miss Maybury exists ... but she does because she's just lit the gas.'

A little light alone in a great expanse of darkness. What *was* she doing there, all alone, year after year?

Sarah prepared to slide down the tree and go home.

And then, suddenly, there wasn't just one light. There were two. The second was some sort of lamp which came bobbing out of the shrubberies on the far side of the grounds.

Sarah froze. She couldn't see who was holding the lamp. It was an unattached glow, a mesmeric, flickering will-o'-the-wisp, weaving its way towards the house.

Who on earth was it, out in the grounds? It couldn't be the old lady. She'd just turned the light on inside.

At the far corner of the house, the light suddenly stopped moving and the person who was carrying it was momentarily silhouetted in its glow. In her astonishment, Sarah almost relaxed her grip on the tree.

It was the silhouette of a slim young man wearing a boater and blazer. The cut of his clothes was exactly the same as was worn by some of the young men in the photographs which she had in her pocket. It was as if one of them had come to life.

The silhouette vanished. The light was moving again. It seemed to flicker its way slowly up the corner of the wall and then disappear at one of the windows. He must have climbed up the ivy.

Unless she'd imagined it? Maybe she had been looking at the photographs so much that she was seeing ghosts now? But she didn't think so.

Her heart was palpitating. Suddenly it seemed to her that the grounds of Lockets and the woods around might be filled with lurking ghosts from the past. She slid down from the tree, switched on her torch and ran just as fast as she was able to through the bramble-choked woods. She had the cringing feeling that someone might be pursuing her, or might step in front of her.

The boys were cycling home in the darkness.

'Still no luck then,' said Rodge, as they paused for a final few words before separating.

'No,' said Tom. 'We'll have to give it a rest tomorrow night, won't we? You two are rowing. Though I could go by myself for a while.'

'We can all have a really long session on Saturday,' said Rodge, 'and then it's going to be the school holidays, anyway.'

Graham was still thoughtful.

'You're still thinking about that girl, aren't you?' said Tom. 'She didn't come back, did she.'

'Probably going for a walk and went back a different way.'

'I just wonder,' said Graham.

*

Sarah was just gratefully retrieving her bike.

By the time she got home she was beginning to regret her panic. Putting her bike away in the shed she hesitated, almost as if she were thinking of riding back.

'Unless I imagined it, there's something funny happening at Lockets,' she thought worriedly. 'Maybe something that *shouldn't* happen. And maybe I should have done something about it instead of running away.'

She didn't know what to do.

3

Sarah Finds an Ally

'Wasn't the lemon pudding vile?' said Gillian, screwing up her face. 'They've dreamed up some masterpieces of horribleness in the school kitchens, but that was really opening up new frontiers –'

'Gillian,' said Sarah. 'Will you or will you not come with me to call on Miss Maybury this evening?'

'Let's be fair, though,' Gillian mused, 'it did take away the taste of the chips.'

'Oh, Gillian!'

Sarah and Gillian were strolling round the school grounds. Sarah had been unable to get Lockets out of her mind all morning.

'Look, Sarah,' said Gillian, with great patience, 'you're obsessed with that place. I'm not. I told you last night I didn't want to go poking round some old ruin inhabited by a crank. So why should it become more appealing when you tell me there's a ghostly figure creeping about with a lantern?'

She rolled her eyes.

'Now you want me to go and knock at the front door!'

'I just have this feeling that I ought to go and speak to the old lady and make sure she's all right.'

'Why shouldn't she be?'

'Well, obviously Gillian ...' Sarah came to a halt. '... maybe I imagined it about the clothes he was wearing but there *was* somebody there. Somebody who waited to see her turn the light on and then got into the house by climbing up the ivy.'

'I'm taking it for granted that you imagined it about the clothes,' said Gillian, 'but I also think you probably imagined the rest as well. Look, you'd been staring at those pictures for ages, then staring at the house. You'd been dreaming about things, imagining things. It's not surprising if your eyes started playing tricks.'

'No, I suppose not. But —'

'But if they weren't and there really is something to bother about, you shouldn't be telling me. You should be telling the police. Or anybody who's bold and fearless and wants to do something about it. But not me.'

Sarah sighed. In different words, that was more or less what her mother had said. Her mother had said she was probably 'romancing again', but if she really was sure then she ought to tell somebody in authority.

But then Mrs Brownbridge probably hadn't really been listening. That was often the case.

'I'd feel silly going to the police,' Sarah replied to Gillian. 'And then they'd probably go along to Lockets and disturb her all for nothing and —'

'There's the bell,' said Gillian, 'the last one of term. Just a bit of clearing up to do and Assembly and we're free for the holidays. Whoopee!'

Sarah couldn't stop thinking about Lockets. She thought about it all afternoon, as they tidied up their desks, as they sat through Assembly, as they burst out of school and scattered to their homes.

'See you soon!' yelled Gillian gaily as she went off in the opposite direction.

Straight after tea, Sarah put on her denim jacket and jeans and got her bike out. She wasn't absolutely sure what she was going to do when she got to Lockets. Maybe she would, after all, find the courage to go and knock on the door herself. But, anyway, she had to go.

At the Private Road sign she knew that she still wasn't brave enough. Kicking herself for her cowardice she parked her bike and set off for the willow tree to have another look at the place before deciding what to do next.

When she came to the spot where she'd met the boys on the previous evening she was reminded of them by the signs of bramble-clearing and she paused to glance round. They really had cut away a lot; much more than was obvious at first sight. It was as if they had tried to disguise how much by leaving the cuttings strewn about. She shrugged her shoulders and walked on.

As she did so, Tom rose silently to his feet. He'd been watching her, crouched behind a bush, since she first came into view.

When she climbed up the willow tree, the house looked just the same. She couldn't imagine why she had thought it might not.

Except, no – it didn't look the same. There wasn't any wisp of smoke from the chimney!

Not that that meant anything, of course. It was a hot day, the sort of day on which very few people would light a fire. On the other hand, it had been warm yesterday and there *had* been smoke.

'Oh dear, I'm working myself into a real state of worry and indecision,' she thought miserably. 'What am I going to do?'

Even if she didn't dare call at the house, it was surely her duty to take a closer look. The least she could do was get into the grounds and see if she could see any sign of life in the house.

There was no possibility of sneaking over the wall, of course. It was much too high. She'd have to go along the private road and enter through the main gates.

Having made her resolve, she scrambled down from the tree at once before she could change her mind and set off to follow the wall. After walking a short distance she thought she heard a twig crackle somewhere behind her. She glanced round but there was nothing to be seen.

'I'm imagining somebody's following me now,' she thought. 'Silly!'

Two or three minutes' walk brought her to the private road just before it passed through the gates of Lockets and became the drive. The large ornate wrought-iron gates had been open so long that ivy was growing up them. The wide, tree-bordered drive curved gently round to her left so that most of the house was hidden from view, only the chimneys peeping up above the trees.

24

Sarah walked in through the gates with mixed emotions. One feeling she had was that she was walking back through time into a different period. Another, more practical, was the awareness that the old lady might be perfectly safe and well and sitting by her window looking along the drive. And if that were the case, by all accounts the batty old lady of Lockets might not take kindly to trespassers.

Nervously, Sarah decided to leave the drive and cut straight towards the house through the shelter of the densely-growing trees. Almost as soon as she'd done so, she found herself in a glade.

It was a lovely big glade and the sunshine streamed into it. It was big enough to take a large Victorian swing and, in the centre, a gnarled old mulberry tree, the trunk of which leaned over and almost touched the ground. It was enchanting, and Sarah halted there.

'If it weren't for my clothes when I look down, I could imagine it's 1914 now,' she thought, 'and when I go out of here all the ladies will be wearing long dresses and wide-brimmed hats and there'll be horse-drawn carts and –'

On one of the trees that surrounded the glade someone had carved, many years ago, a heart with an arrow through it. On either side of it were the initials E.C. and C.A.M.

Sarah found that little carving so sweet and touching that it brought a lump to her throat. Then the significance of the initials struck her.

C.A.M.! Those were the old lady's initials!

Maybe she was the batty old lady of Lockets now but once upon a time, many years ago, she had been in this glade in the sunshine while someone had romantically carved her initials on a tree.

'I wonder who "E.C." was?' she thought, 'and what happened to him?'

She sat down on the swing and pushed at the ground with her feet. She was finding this place so magical that for a few moments she had forgotten what had brought her here. She had that entranced, wistful, yearning feeling again ...

This time there was no mistake about it. She *had* heard

the rustle of leaves and the crackle of twigs underfoot. Someone was coming stealthily towards the glade.

There wasn't time to jump off the swing and run. She clutched the chains hard, put her feet on the ground, and waited. Visions of that lantern, of the silhouetted boater and blazer were leaping into her mind.

But it was the modern world that arrived. It was the fair-haired boy who stood looking at her from the edge of the glade.

Sarah found she was trembling with a mixture of relief and indignation. She jumped to her feet.

'You've been following me, haven't you,' she said. 'You followed me here from the wood. That's what I heard.'

Tom gave a slow, embarrassed smile. He nodded.

'Why?'

'I wondered what you were up to,' he said. 'You have been behaving pretty peculiarly, haven't you? You've been sneaking around the place as if you were going to break in.'

Sarah stared at him.

'I suppose you're right,' she said, mollified. She'd found before that it was hard to remain indignant with him. She sat down on the swing again.

'You don't really believe that, do you?' she asked a little anxiously. 'That I was going to break in?'

Tom laughed. 'No,' he said, 'but I would like to know what you are up to, even if I am being nosy.'

He wasn't being entirely open with her. He'd really started to follow her because he'd wanted to find out if there were anything in Graham's suspicions. But he couldn't tell her that. And, anyway, he'd been growing steadily more intrigued.

Sarah hesitated. She'd never even spoken to him properly before, but she liked the look of him and here he was, actually taking an interest. Nobody else had. And she needed someone to confide in.

'I'm worried,' she said, 'about the old lady who lives in this house.'

Tom sat down on the mulberry tree.

26

'I'm interested,' he said. 'Tell me.'

He listened patiently as she told him about the pictures and how, because of them, she'd come to look at Lockets. He wasn't flip or cynical as Gillian or Corinne might have been. When she told him about the ghostly figure he looked startled and was obviously wondering whether she were making it up, but a glance at her face seemed to convince him.'

'That's really peculiar,' he said, when she'd finished. 'What do you think it was you saw? Do you believe in ghosts?'

'Well, no, of course not but – I'm just baffled. I don't *think* I imagined things.'

'Have you got those pictures with you?' he asked. 'I'd like to see them if you have.'

She took them from her pocket, got up from the swing and handed them to him wordlessly, then sat down again.

He studied each picture closely, looking at the date on the envelope and then said:

'You mean these were taken here, in the grounds of this house?'

'On the lawns by the river.'

She could tell they meant something to him, too.

'You must have been really taken with these,' he said. 'Fascinated. After I'd first looked at them, I walked along the street and everything in the present seemed so – so drab. I can't explain it, but when I looked at the pictures again they seemed like a wonderful, remote world where there was romance and mystery and adventure –'

'You're romantic,' said Tom. But he didn't say it as if it were an insult. 'You think the past was romantic because it's out of reach. But I don't suppose it really was. You're fascinated by something that never existed.'

'But it does exist,' said Sarah. 'In these pictures ... in the atmosphere in this glade ...'

He grinned. 'I agree with you,' he said. 'But I suppose that's because I'm romantic as well.'

He got up and put the pictures back on her lap. Then, thoughtfully, he gave the swing a push.

27

'Perhaps we should show them to the batty old lady of Lockets,' he said. 'She might be interested in them.'

Sarah looked round at him eagerly. 'You mean – ?'

'I think we ought to make sure she's all right. And tell her she had a visitor last night. If you don't mind me muscling in, that is.'

'Mind!' Sarah jumped off the swing. 'Let's go now before you have second thoughts.' She was already finding him very easy to talk to, as though he were an old friend.

'I won't have second thoughts,' he said. 'My name's Tom Riddings, by the way. What's yours?'

'Sarah Brownbridge and I live in Cherringham.'

To have an ally! It seemed to Sarah that something magical had taken place within a few minutes in that glade. She had entered it alone, scared, not knowing what to do. Now she was feeling entirely different and all because she had met someone whose mind seemed to run on the same lines as her own.

Just one thing, though. 'I've told you everything I've been doing,' she said. 'What about telling me what *you* were doing last night?'

He had the grace to be embarrassed.

'Sorry,' he said. 'I can't. That isn't only my secret.'

She laughed. It didn't really matter. She pointed out the carving on the tree to him and then they set off towards the house.

As they emerged from the trees, there was no angry face at the window, no threatening shout, only stillness.

The big lion's head knocker hadn't been used for many years and it was stiff. Tom had to bang very hard to make it work and the blows seemed to thunder and echo inside the house, reverberating round the strange little world of Miss Constance Maybury.

28

4

Inside Lockets

Nothing happened.

'Are you *sure* somebody lives here?' asked Tom, perplexed, after he had wielded the knocker for the third time.

'Well, she's supposed to be a recluse,' said Sarah, anxiously. 'Maybe she just isn't answering the door. Or maybe she's out of earshot at the other end of the house. Or maybe –'

She didn't like to think of anything else.

'Maybe something did happen to her last night,' said Tom, who wasn't so squeamish.

'Do you think we should try and get inside and see?' asked Sarah.

'Don't be daft. We'd be breaking and entering. If we think something's wrong, we'd better go and report it.'

'Let me have one last go,' said Sarah.

'You'll have the door down if you thump like that,' said Tom.

But the noise reverberated away – and still nothing.

'I suppose we may as well give up and go,' she said, turning away sadly. 'Do you really think we should tell the police?'

She'd been keyed up waiting for the door to open and now that she'd given up hope she felt a sense of loss, as well as being worried.

Then suddenly she froze, listening.

'Can you hear something?' she said.

'Yes,' said Tom. 'A tapping sound. It's a walking stick!'

The flap of the letter box clicked open.

'Who is that?' said a voice.

It was the voice of an old lady but it wasn't at all

29

quavery. Nor did it sound in the least 'batty'. It was a calm, sweet voice and there was even, thought Sarah, a touch of nervous eagerness in it, as if she'd been waiting hopefully for a visitor.

'I'm sorry if we're disturbing you,' Sarah said to the letter-box. 'My name's Sarah Brownbridge, and this is Tom Riddings –'

'I'm sorry,' said the voice. The eagerness had disappeared from it and it sounded flat – 'but I am not at home to callers nowadays.'

The flap clicked shut.

Sarah and Tom looked at each other, disconcerted.

'That was telling us straight,' said Tom.

They could hear the stick tap-tapping away again.

'Well, she seems to be all right, anyway,' said Sarah. 'That's a big relief.'

'We may as well go,' said Tom, and he turned away.

And then, from inside the house, they heard a cry.

'She's fallen!' cried Sarah. Before Tom could get to the letter box she was pushing back the flap and peering through.

She could see a long, heavily-furnished, rather dark hall with a wide staircase leading up from it.

At the far end of the hall there seemed to be two or three steps going down. Sarah could just make out what looked like a huddled heap.

'Can you see her?' Tom was asking.

'I think that's her, lying there. Looks as if she fell going down some steps. Oh, it's my fault for calling.'

Tom pushed at the door but it didn't budge. 'Let's see if we can get in through a window,' he said. He ran out of the porch.

'But won't that be breaking and entering?' gasped Sarah, as she ran after him.

'We can't leave her lying there.'

The windows were of the Victorian sash type and the first one they came to was slightly ajar at the top.

'The catch is off,' said Tom with relief. 'At least we don't have to break it. It's just a question of pushing the bottom up. Both together ... now!'

It shot up at the first heave and they scrambled through.

They were in a large, high-ceilinged sitting-room. The furniture was Victorian or Edwardian and darkly gleaming. That was Sarah's first surprise. She'd expected everything to be as neglected inside as the house appeared from the outside, but it wasn't. There was a pleasant smell of furniture polish and a large portrait looked at her from the opposite end of the room.

Sarah took all that in at a glance before following Tom through a door and into the hall. She was thinking that she would never have dared do this on her own. She was about to confront the batty old lady of Lockets.

Batty old lady of Lockets, indeed!

Miss Maybury was trying to get up, her face turned towards them. Sarah instantly thought it was the sweetest face she had ever seen. She wore a white blouse and a long, dark skirt buttoned down the front which certainly wasn't this year's fashion. Her walking stick lay near her.

She obviously wasn't in any great pain. She wore, rather, an expression of vexation at her helplessness and timidity at the sight of them. Yes, timidity.

'Are you hurt?' asked Sarah, as she and Tom knelt down beside her.

'It's my ankle,' said Miss Maybury. 'I can't put any weight on it for the moment. Perhaps if you could reach me my stick?'

Tom put it in her hand. 'We'll help you to a chair,' he said.

Helping her along the hall, Sarah was amazed to discover how light she was. She was slim and erect and no bigger than Sarah herself. She was very old and her hair was white but she had clearly once been very beautiful. In fact, thought Sarah, she still was.

They helped her into the room they had passed through and after they had placed her in an armchair, Tom went over and closed the window. Miss Maybury watched him, recovering.

'Thank you,' she said. She was still breathing hard, but

she was smiling. 'I suppose you children think I'm a helpless old woman who shouldn't be on her own. I can assure you I'm perfectly capable. An accident like this could happen to anyone.'

'Should we make you a cup of tea?' asked Sarah, who *had* been thinking something like that.

'No thank you,' said Miss Maybury. 'You've been very kind to come in and help me, but ...'

She was looking Sarah up and down, taking in her clothes – the denim jacket, the jeans, the cheesecloth blouse – as if she had never seen such things before.

'... but I think you should go now. As I told you, I am not at home to callers nowadays!'

'I'm sorry, Miss Maybury,' said Sarah firmly, 'but we insist. Don't we, Tom?'

'We do,' confirmed Tom.

Sarah wasn't in the least scared any more. Having got into the house by a fluke she wasn't going to be driven off quite so rapidly.

'Just you rest while we find the kitchen; you're looking better already.'

Sarah and Tom were out in the hall again before Miss Maybury could object further. Tom was looking preoccupied. 'You find the kitchen,' he whispered, 'and I'll be with you in a couple of minutes. I want to have a quick look around.'

The kitchen was at the back of the house down a few stone steps. Sarah lit an ancient gas ring with a match from the box that was lying on the wooden draining board and filled the heavy kettle.

As soon as she'd put it on, she took the pictures from her pocket and selected the one of the young girl.

'It *is* her,' she whispered. 'I'm *sure* it's Miss Maybury.'

It wasn't any particular feature that made Sarah so positive. It was the expression that had remained the same, the wonderfully sweet expression.

'They don't make faces as sweet as that any more,' thought Sarah. 'Faces are different nowadays.'

'But what was she looking at that day in 1914? I wonder

if she'd remember if I asked her?'

Just then Tom came in. He was holding a newspaper.

'Have you noticed anything surprising about this house?' he asked.

'Miss Maybury's the biggest surprise,' said Sarah. 'All these rumours about a crank living here ... a batty old lady ... I was expecting some sort of wild woman and she's – well, she's lovely, isn't she?'

She showed Tom the picture.

'Yes, it's her all right,' said Tom. He seemed fascinated, but still preoccupied as he handed it back to her.

'There is something peculiar about Miss Maybury, though. Have you noticed that there's nothing in this house later than about 1914?'

Sarah frowned, casting her mind back. 'Her clothes? I noticed that straight away. That *was* surprising. And there's no modern furniture, but I suppose that's to be expected –'

'But this isn't to be expected,' said Tom. He held out the newspaper.

It wasn't a newspaper that Sarah had seen before and the date on it was Monday, 3rd August, 1914.

It was lying on the hallstand as if it had just arrived,' said Tom. 'There are other newspapers and magazines there as well – all around the same date.'

'Around the date of the garden party,' said Sarah softly. 'Look!' She was gazing at a calendar on the wall. It was for the year 1914 and the month exposed was August.

'You're right,' she said. 'There isn't anything here later than that.'

'It's as if the clock suddenly stopped,' said Tom. 'I half expect to look down and see myself in a sailor suit or whatever it was boys wore then.'

The kettle was boiling.

'Anyway,' said Sarah, 'we'd better take Miss Maybury her tea and tell her what I saw last night. I don't want to alarm her, but I think she ought to know. Don't you?'

'Yes, I do,' said Tom.

Sarah put four spoonfuls of tea into the pot, from a

caddy she found on the shelf, and poured on the water while Tom produced three large willow-pattern cups and saucers.

'I'll carry the tray for you,' he said, as she poured. He was still looking thoughtful.

It was funny to think she and Tom hadn't even known each other half an hour ago. Here they were, whispering and conspiring together and helping each other as if they were old friends.

Miss Maybury was still sitting in the same place when they returned. She seemed to be gazing dreamily at the portrait which Sarah had noticed when she first entered.

'Yes,' thought Sarah, 'the clothes she's wearing are definitely first world war or before.' And there was nothing modern to be seen – nothing.

'Tea, Miss Maybury,' said Tom, brightly. He gave Sarah the tray to hold while he pulled a small table towards the old lady.

While he was doing so, Sarah looked at the portrait herself. It was of a dazzlingly handsome young man with the face of a Greek god. His mass of shining golden hair was cut much longer than would have been fashionable in his day because it was clear from his collar and tie that his day had been the same as Miss Maybury's.

And then Sarah noticed the name on the little brass plate beneath the portrait. EDMUND COPE.

Edmund Cope! Initials E.C.! The initials carved on the tree. Was he the person who'd done the carving then?

But the name Edmund Cope meant something else to her, too. She'd learned about him at school. Surely he'd been a poet, killed in the first world war – !

'You can put the tray down now, Sarah,' said Tom.

As she did so, Sarah noticed that Miss Maybury was now watching her closely with what looked to be a rather wistful expression on her face. Then the old lady picked up her tea and smiled faintly.

'Thank you,' she said. 'I've noticed that you know my name. Why don't you both sit down and tell me why you've come?'

Sarah and Tom each took an armchair, rather self-consciously.

'Well, you see –' began Sarah. Then she stopped. Suddenly it all seemed very silly.

What was she trying to do? she wondered. Alarm the old lady over nothing? She'd probably imagined it all last night.

'It's – well – it's –' Then suddenly it came out in a rush. 'It's probably stupid but I've been worried that somebody might be getting into your house. I thought I saw somebody last night –'

Miss Maybury got to her feet with an effort. She didn't look in the least alarmed. Rather it seemed she had to make a movement to release a tremor of excitement which ran through her.

'Oh, but someone *is* coming into the house at night,' she said. 'I've heard him – several times, always upstairs.'

Her gaze was fixed on the portrait of Edmund Cope.

5

Tom's Invitation

'You mean you *know*,' said Tom, 'and you don't mind?'

But Miss Maybury was looking at Sarah again. There was a sort of pathetic eagerness about her.

'Tell me – did you happen to see what this – this person looked like?'

'Well,' said Sarah, weakly, 'I – I sort of *thought* I saw a silhouette of somebody but I expect I just imagined it. I mean ... it looked like a man wearing clothes from – well, sort of Edwardian clothes – a boater and so on.'

She stopped. Miss Maybury was looking at the portrait again with that look of repressed excitement.

'But,' persisted Tom, 'if you think somebody's breaking into the house, then surely we ought to tell the police.'

'Oh, no,' said Miss Maybury, suddenly moved to alarm. She looked round at him. 'You mustn't do that. Promise me you won't.'

'But –'

'Please,' said Miss Maybury, 'both of you, *please* promise.'

'All – all right,' said Sarah helplessly.

'I promise,' she and Tom drawled out sheepishly in unison.

'And now,' said Miss Maybury, 'I think you should go. Thank you for what you've told me and for helping me. I do appreciate it but I'm really not used to visitors, you know.'

'Your ankle –' said Sarah.

'It's better now,' said Miss Maybury. 'Look, I'll show you.'

She walked a few paces and then stood there smiling at them. It was a smile of great charm and Sarah was vividly reminded of that young girl back in 1914.

'Well, before we go,' said Sarah, 'at least let me take the cups back to the kitchen and wash them up.' And before the old lady could object she put them on the tray and hurried out.

She wanted to escape from Miss Maybury for a few moments because she was dying to have a look upstairs, even if necessarily a very brief one. If someone was getting in there regularly she might just get an idea why.

She washed up the cups and saucers very quickly then raced on tiptoe along the hall, swung round the post at the foot of the stairs and darted up them. As she did so, dust started rising from the stair carpet.

At the top of the stairs she halted, looking along a long corridor. Downstairs, the rooms she had seen had been well cared-for, the furniture gleaming. Not so here.

Great swathes of cobwebs hung across the corridor and the dust was thick everywhere. Although there were windows at each end, they let in very little light because of the foliage which had grown unchecked outside them.

'Of course,' thought Sarah, appalled, 'she can't get up here to clean. I don't suppose anybody's been up here in years except ...'

Overpowered by it, she fled downstairs.

Miss Maybury was sitting down, apparently sunk in thought, when Sarah re-entered the sitting room but she immediately rose to her feet again.

'I shall see you out,' she said.

The front door was locked with a large key which obviously hadn't been turned for many years. Miss Maybury watched as Tom forced it round and then opened the door and Sarah thought how strange it must seem to the old lady to be showing out visitors. When last had she seen the view through the open doorway?

Sarah stood in the porch beside Tom, plucking up her courage.

'Would you mind,' she said timidly to the old lady, 'if we – if I were to come and visit you again?'

She was expecting an immediate refusal but it was a moment before Miss Maybury replied. She was looking at Sarah with that slightly wistful expression on her face again.

'No,' she said. 'I told you that I don't receive visitors.'

To Sarah's surprise there seemed a hint of regret in her voice. It gave her the courage to try again.

'I'd like to help you tidy up a little – some of the places you can't get to – like upstairs. And I'd like to help you find out what this person is doing upstairs when he comes –'

From the eager expression that flitted across Miss Maybury's face it was clear that Sarah had struck a chord.

'I can't think why you should want to come and see an old woman like me,' she said, 'but if you do ... well ... perhaps ... sometime ...'

The door closed, leaving Sarah and Tom staring at it, side by side. Then they looked at each other.

'Extraordinary place!' said Tom.

'Did you see the way she looked at that portrait?' said Sarah. 'And the way she got excited when I told her that the man last night was wearing sort of Edwardian clothes –'

'She thinks it's *him* who's getting into the house, doesn't she? The chap in the portrait.'

'That's what it looked like,' said Sarah. 'But did you realise who the portrait's of? It's Edmund Cope, the poet –'

'Edmund Cope! Of course,' said Tom, snapping his fingers together. 'I knew I recognised the name. We've learned about him in English.'

'Then you'll remember he was killed in the first world war. He's been dead over sixty years.'

Miss Maybury walked slowly along the hall to the back of the house and entered the dining room. The highly polished table was laid for two and there were candles on it waiting to be lit.

It had been very strange and exhausting for her to have those two young visitors in the house. She ought really to have insisted that they go immediately, but she hadn't been able to do that.

She had found it fascinating to watch the girl, in particular. Somehow it brought back memories of her own girl-hood. Her face was so open, honest, trusting – an old-fashioned sort of face.

But now she wanted to get back into her routine. By the french windows overlooking the lawn was a chair and Miss Maybury sat down on it. From there she could look out across the overgrown lawns to the broken jetty and the rotting boathouses.

Except that to Miss Maybury they weren't overgrown, broken and rotting. As she peered out rather short-sightedly into the warm sunshine, she saw it as it had been many years ago.

She seemed to be waiting for someone.

'So although she seems so nice, she really is a bit batty,' said Tom.

He and Sarah were walking slowly down the drive.

'Perhaps I am, too, then,' said Sarah, 'because what I saw ... well –' she glanced at Tom defensively, 'when I come to think of it, the person I saw *could* have been him.'

'Even if he were alive now he'd be over eighty years old and not up to climbing ivy,' Tom pointed out, 'and since he isn't ...'

'Then who was it? And even if I imagined it, why should I have imagined somebody who looked like Edmund Cope?'

'I don't know,' said Tom. 'The whole thing's peculiar.' He added, very quietly : 'And somebody *is* getting into the house.'

At the gates they paused to look back at the house.

'What do you know about Edmund Cope?' asked Tom.

'Not much. I know he was very good-looking. Like a Greek god.'

'And Miss Maybury knew him?'

'She must have done if he carved those initials on the tree,' said Sarah. 'And now she's living in a house where the clock stopped in 1914, imagining that he's breaking into it ...'

39

Sarah suddenly remembered something. 'After all that,' she said, 'I didn't even show her the pictures.'

'I'd better get going,' said Tom abruptly. 'I haven't eaten yet. My bike's down there.' He pointed along the private road.

'So's mine,' said Sarah. It suddenly dawned upon her that the time was approaching when she and Tom would go their separate ways. She had felt that the events of the last hour had made them old friends, but obviously there wasn't any reason why he should feel the same. The thought depressed her.

'I was wondering,' she said rather timidly, 'whether it would be worth waiting to see if anybody comes again tonight.'

She was hoping that Tom would offer to join her, but all he said was : 'I wouldn't if I were you. Come on.' Then he set off to walk along the private road. She followed. She had no intention of staying by herself.

Their bikes turned out to be within a few yards of each other.

'I live in Enslow,' he said. 'We can ride together till we reach the main road.'

Enslow was the next little town along the river from Cherringham. They were only two or three miles apart.

Tom didn't speak as they rode along. He seemed to be turning something over in his mind.

As they drew near the main road, the sight of a modern house with a car standing in the drive gave Sarah a feeling of incredulity for a moment, because she was still mentally at Lockets in 1914.

She was puzzled by Tom's silence. She wanted to talk about what they'd seen and she'd expected that he would, too. And if he wasn't going to be interested any more, what was she going to do about Miss Maybury?

For she knew that she wasn't simply going to be able to forget about Miss Maybury now. She had to know what was going on at Lockets. But she couldn't do that by herself. She had to have help. And it wouldn't come from Gillian.

At the main road, Tom pulled into the side and stopped and put his feet on the ground. Sarah followed suit.

'I've made up my mind,' said Tom.

'About what?'

'This mystery you've uncovered at Lockets,' said Tom. 'It's the most exciting thing I've come across. It's yours – you discovered it – but I think you're going to need help, aren't you.'

'A lot,' said Sarah, spirits lifting.

'Besides,' said Tom, almost to himself, 'you'd fit in all right. You're the first outsider I've met who would.'

'What do you mean?' asked Sarah, mystified, though it sounded flattering.

'I'm talking about the Clover Club. It's a club that Graham and Rodge and I formed, just the three of us, to go out and *look* for adventure because we feel that, if you don't, nothing ever happens nowadays.'

'That's a bit the way I feel myself,' said Sarah.

'Well, you've looked for one and come up with a grade A1 top exhibit. What I'm suggesting –' Tom hesitated for just a moment and then went on – 'I'm suggesting that you become a sort of temporary member of the Clover Club and that this business of Edmund Cope becomes a club affair.'

'That'd be marvellous,' said Sarah eagerly, 'as long as the others would agree.'

'It'll have to be decided by a vote,' said Tom, 'but I should think they'll jump at it – I wouldn't have said anything about it if I didn't think that. We're having a meeting at our HQ tomorrow morning at ten o'clock. Can you come?'

'Where is it?'

From his pocket, Tom produced a notebook and ball-point pen. Then he hesitated again.

'Promise you'll keep this secret? We don't want anybody else muscling in on our HQ,' he said.

'I promise faithfully.'

He looked at her. 'I trust you absolutely,' he said. He started to draw in the notebook.

'This is a plan showing how to get there from Cherringham. It's not far. You see, I live in Enslow, Graham at Madford and Rodge lives more or less in between. His father's a farmer so we use an old building that belongs to him. It's stuck away all by itself.'

He tore the page from the notebook and handed it to her.

'There you are. It's a small brick building.'

'What sort of building? A cottage?'

Tom laughed. 'Well, to be honest, it's been used as a pig sty among other things. The cottage that was with it fell down long ago – it used to be called Clover Cottage, that's why we call ourselves the Clover Club. But the sty's still there. There haven't been any pigs in it for a long time though, not real ones anyway.'

He lifted his foot to the pedal, preparing to go.

'Tomorrow we'll discuss everything and if the others agree we'll decide on a plan of action. Miss Maybury doesn't want the outside world moving into Lockets but I think she'll accept us if you're there. I could tell she was really taken by you.'

'I liked her,' said Sarah.

'One other thing. There's no use waiting till after the meeting before we get things moving. Will you be responsible for going to the library first thing tomorrow and finding out all you can about Edmund Cope?'

'Leave it to me,' said Sarah.

'Oh, and one last thing,' said Tom. 'When you get to the HQ tomorrow we have a special knock. Two short and two longs.'

It had been a day of many wonders, thought Sarah as she cycled home. Here amidst Cherringham's traffic, Lockets itself seemed impossibly remote, a house in another age as if she'd passed through a science-fiction time-lock.

As darkness fell at Lockets, Miss Maybury rose from her chair and lit the gaslight as she did every evening. Then she sat down again and dozed.

Some time later she woke and raised her head, listening. Taking her stick, she opened the dining room door and walked along the hall which was illuminated only by the dim glow of the gaslight through the open door. She was looking up at the ceiling.

'Edmund,' she called. 'Edmund!'

She halted by the banisters, gazing upwards beseechingly. From somewhere upstairs came the distant sound of a closing door and the soft pad of footsteps.

'Edmund, answer me, please. Is that you?'

Something white came fluttering down between the banisters and fell at her feet. It was something familiar – something that stirred memories of many years ago. She stooped and picked it up.

6

A Clover Club Quarrel

Sarah was waiting outside the public library when the doors opened the next morning. She had woken early, full of excitement at the prospect of joining up with the Clover Club and finding out what was going on at Lockets.

There was only one book of interest. It contained Edmund Cope's collected poems, but nothing about his life. She glanced at some of the earlier poems. They were mostly about the countryside, very simple and direct. She liked them.

As she got it stamped she asked Mrs Ridgway, the librarian, if she happened to know anything about Edmund Cope.

'Not a lot,' admitted Mrs Ridgway, 'except that he was very good-looking and used to make all the ladies swoon when he passed by. And that he had connections with this area. He lived somewhere near Hamblesey for a while.'

Hamblesey was the largest of the riverside towns. It wasn't far away. It *could* have been Edmund Cope himself who'd carved his initials on that tree!

'Just a moment,' said Mrs Ridgway, as Sarah was turning away. She went over to a small drawer and flicked through some cards. 'Yes, I thought so. There's an Edmund Cope society in Hamblesey. They read his poetry and have discussions about him and so on! They could give you some information if you really want it. Would you like the secretary's name and address?'

Sarah said she would and the librarian wrote them on a piece of paper for her. Then, with the book in her pocket, Sarah set off to find Clover Club HQ. She felt a bit like someone off on a secret mission.

She found the HQ close to the main river, down a

short lane leading from the road, built of brick as Tom had said, with a proper door and two windows which were so encrusted with dirt that it was impossible to see through them. It was high enough to have two floors, the upper of which had probably been a hay loft – it had obviously once been the outbuilding of a farm labourer's cottage which had been pulled down and the garden taken back into agriculture.

It stood now in the corner of a field, still partly surrounded by shrubs from the original garden and some of the original wall.

Clover Club HQ!

There was no obvious sign that the place was other than deserted, but round the back Sarah found two bikes parked and she put her own with them. Presumably there was a third somewhere nearby and the boys were inside. It was a quarter past ten. She'd deliberately arrived a little late so as to give Tom the chance to explain the situation to the other boys first.

She went round to the door and hesitated in front of it for a moment, suddenly nervous. But she couldn't afford to have nerves. She needed the Clover Club. She raised her hand.

Just like Tom had said, two short knocks and two long ones.

Almost before she had finished, there was the sound of a key turning stiffly in the lock and the door was pulled open to reveal one of the boys she had seen in the wood. It was the dark-haired, rather gloomy looking one but he wasn't looking gloomy now. He was smiling quite dazzlingly.

'Hallo, Tom,' he was saying. 'You're late.'

And then, as he took in who was standing there, his smile faded, giving way to the most complete look of outraged astonishment that Sarah had ever seen.

'What on earth –! What are *you* doing here?'

It was an awful moment. Tom wasn't there!

She could see inside. Scattered about the flagstoned floor were a few tattered old cushions, the only furnishings, and

45

on one of them was sitting the third boy, arms round his
knees, looking at her in a sort of solemn disbelief as if she
couldn't be real. The walls were covered with pictures
cut out from magazines, mostly of aeroplanes as far as
she could see. And that was the total contents. No Tom.
He hadn't arrived yet. She hadn't been expected.

'How,' demanded the enraged Graham, 'do you know
our knock?'

'Because I told her, Graham. Calm down,' said a voice
from behind and, turning, Sarah saw to her immense relief
that Tom was getting off his bike behind her. She'd been
so frozen with embarrassment that she hadn't heard him
turn in.

He looked just as embarrassed. He was panting as if he'd
been riding very hard.

'Sorry, Sarah – got a puncture today of all days – had
meant to get here first –'

'You – you told her?' Graham was saying incredulously.

'Calm down, Graham,' said Tom again hastily as he
propped his bike behind a shrub. 'Let's all go inside and
I'll explain.'

It was an unfortunate start, so unfortunate that Sarah
was almost tempted to tell Tom that she'd changed her
mind and didn't want to join the Clover Club after all.

But she did need the Clover Club and she couldn't really
blame Graham. It must have been a shock for him to find
her there. She allowed herself to be ushered inside.

'Sarah ... Graham ... Rodge ...' said Tom, heartily,
obviously trying to take the chill out of the air. He locked
the door behind him again. Rodge had got to his feet and
he nodded, looking friendly. Graham just look puzzled.

'And this is our HQ,' said Tom. 'Not bad, is it.'

Sarah looked around. The 'room' she was in occupied
most of the floor space of the little building but another
smaller 'room' could be glimpsed through a gap in the
dividing wall. She could see that a ladder led up from there
to the loft.

The pictures on the wall were not entirely of military

aircraft. For variety, there were a few of tanks and warships, a sprinkling of sportsmen and some of a rowing crew standing by their boat.

The windows were too dirty to let much light through and Sarah longed to take a cloth to them. The floor was strewn with bits of chocolate wrappers, toffee papers and other litter. The whole atmosphere was, she thought, all in all and to put it mildly, masculine.

'It could be marvellous,' she said, and she meant it. She was thinking how nice it would be to clean it up and put curtains at the window and a carpet down.

'Graham may not have learned much history at school but ask him which pilot flew the most missions on the western front in Christmas week 1917 and I expect he'd give you the answer in a flash.'

But Tom's gentle teasing didn't seem to be softening Graham at all.

'What's all this about, Tom?' he asked.

'Yes, to business,' said Tom. 'Everybody had better take a cushion.'

Sarah sat down as did the others. She was again wondering whether she shouldn't just go, but Tom flashed her a meaning glance as if to warn her against it.

'I invited Sarah here with the idea of her being voted a temporary member of the Clover Club' – Sarah saw the startled look that appeared on Graham's face – 'and before any member says I had no right to do that without discussing it first – all right, I hadn't. But I was sure you'd feel the same way as I do, and I still am.'

Tom told them all that Sarah and he had seen and heard at Lockets. When he'd finished he turned to Sarah. 'Anything else to say?' he asked her.

Sarah had been watching the other two. Rodge had listened with great interest and the occasional exclamation. Graham's face had remained stony, as if to show an interest would be a sign of weakness.

'When Tom said it would be a good idea for me to come, I jumped at it,' she said. 'But I don't want to cause any rows. If you don't want me I'll go away again. But I am bothered about Miss Maybury. I think she might need help and I'm not much use to her alone.'

Graham was looking stubbornly at his shoes. 'I think she should wait outside while we talk about it and take a vote,' he said.

'Fair enough, don't you think, Sarah?' said Tom. But he looked taken aback.

'Of course it is,' said Sarah. She got up and Tom unlocked the door for her.

'See you in a minute,' he hissed after she had gone outside. 'Graham's nice really. You'll like him once you get to know him.' He winked at her before closing the door again.

Sarah stood there feeling a complete idiot. From inside, faintly, she heard Tom's voice.

'What's the matter? We'd be stupid not to follow up an adventure like this. And I like her – she's one of us –'

And then, killingly, another voice, Graham's: 'Tom, you're not getting the message. Rodge and I don't want her.'

It was humiliating. But she couldn't blame Graham if that was the way he felt. In fact she liked him. There was a look of stubborn honesty about him which appealed to her.

She moved a little further away so as not to eavesdrop. Apart from being bad manners it might also prove painful.

'But why,' Tom was saying, '*why?*'

'I can think of at least five good reasons,' said Graham. 'To start with, Rodge and I have only seen her once before and then she seemed to be spying on us.'

'She wasn't Graham. That's why I followed her in the first place, to find out what she was up to. And she knows nothing about what we're doing.'

'Second, we've got the big job on hand for the Skipper. We can't let anything interfere with that.'

'It won't, Graham. It's the school holidays now. We've got plenty of time.'

'Thirdly, I don't believe half this story anyway. We've

48

only got her word for it she saw this ghostly figure.'

'You haven't been to the house, Graham – I have, and I believe it!'

'Fourth, poets and old ladies aren't in my line. They don't excite me and fifth, the Clover Club is for *boys*.'

'And that's the real reason, isn't it?' cried Tom. He paced up and down clutching at the air despairingly. 'We've got women pilots and judges and goodness knows what, but we can't have a girl in the Clover Club.'

'That,' said Graham, 'is right. The rot stops here. And I know Rodge will agree with me even if he has lost his voice this morning.'

Outside, Sarah made up her mind, even though she'd heard none of this.

'It's going to be so embarrassing,' she thought. 'Tom's going to come out through that door in a minute, not able to look me in the eye, and tell me that I can't be a member of the Clover Club, after all. And I'll have to say, "Well, not to worry – nice of you to ask me but I wasn't really bothered – just a sort of idle whim, really". And then I'll have to get on my bike and ride away with dignity, whistling cheerfully if I can manage it.'

She moved towards her bike.

'Much better if I can save all that. He'll be so relieved to find I've just disappeared when he comes out.'

While, inside:

'All right,' said Tom, wearily, 'there's no point in arguing any more. Let's put it to the vote. Those in favour of Sarah Brownbridge becoming a temporary member of the Clover Club, raise their hands.'

He raised his own hand firmly. Equally firmly, Graham folded his arms. They both looked at Rodge.

Sarah was just pausing at the main road when she heard shouts behind her. She looked round to see Tom speeding after her on his bike.

'What's the matter?' he panted, pulling up beside her. 'Don't you *want* to be a member of the Clover Club?'

She looked at him in disbelief.

'You mean –?'

49

It was clear from the look of elation on his face what he meant. He knew why she'd gone as well, that was obvious.

'Come on,' he said, 'you're holding up business.'

But she hesitated. 'Tom, are you sure,' she said. 'I mean, did everybody vote for me or –'

'That's none of your business,' he said. 'A vote is a vote and it's binding on all members. Rule 17c of the Clover Club. It's of no interest to anyone afterwards whether it's unanimous or not. Now come on and stop wasting time.'

Graham and Rodge were standing up when Tom ushered her into HQ again. 'This is an historic moment,' he said. 'The Clover Club welcomes its first lady member.'

'Temporary member,' Graham corrected him, impassively.

'Welcome,' said Rodge, speaking the first word that Sarah had heard him deliver that morning. His left eye closed slowly in a large, solemn wink and then he grinned at her.

'Welcome,' said Graham, still impassive.

'Just one condition that I know you won't mind,' said Tom. 'As a temporary member you'll be admitted into certain secrets like where we hide the key to HQ, but there are some things you won't be allowed to know. For instance you won't be told anything about the other job we've got on hand.'

Sarah quickly decided to hide her disappointment over that.

Tom rubbed his hands. 'Right, then. Everybody sit down and we'll decide on what our first move is as far as the mystery of Lockets is concerned.'

At Lockets that morning Miss Maybury was sitting in her usual place by the dining-room windows. She was twisting a handkerchief in her hands and she kept looking down at it, her expression a mixture of excitement and incredulity.

It was a man's handkerchief, very fine, of linen, and embroidered on it were the initials E.C.

'Oh, Edmund,' she whispered. 'One of the handkerchiefs I embroidered for you. It's a sign from you. Now I know you have come back.'

Tenderly she folded the handkerchief and put it in her belt.

7

A Mission for Sarah

'The first thing is to have a proper look round upstairs,' said Sarah. 'I wouldn't have the nerve to go up there again by myself but with all of us there, we might find some clue as to what's going on.'

Sarah and the boys were planning their first moves at Lockets.

'Would this old lady – Miss Maybury – let us?' asked Rodge. He was taking a keen interest and Sarah could see that he was excited.

'I think she would,' said Tom. 'She really seemed to brighten up when Sarah mentioned it.'

'I'd like to clean up the place for her a bit, too,' said Sarah, 'the grounds as well. I think she'd like that.'

Sarah was thinking she'd like it, too. To see Lockets beautiful again as it had been in those pictures ...

'What we've got to aim for, of course,' said Tom practically, 'is to get on the track of whoever is breaking in and find out who it is. But we can think of the best way of doing that after we've had a look upstairs as Sarah says. When should we go there, then. Today?'

'Can't,' said Graham. 'We've got to get on with the Skipper's project today.'

Graham was remaining impassively correct in his attitude to Sarah. She hadn't any doubt that he had voted against her joining the club and was now making the best of it. It rather took the gilt off the gingerbread because if it hadn't been for that she'd have been revelling in being a member and making plans.

'What about tomorrow morning, then?' said Tom.

'Sunday. Rodge and I have got rowing practice,' said Graham promptly.

'Oh, yes,' Tom glanced at Sarah. 'Graham and Rodge both belong to Madford Rowing Club Juniors,' he explained. 'You might say they're Madfordly keen on it. We'll have to make it tomorrow afternoon, then. Meet at the private road sign outside Lockets at three o'clock.

'Just one other thing. Since we're tied up today, you'd better go and see this Edmund Cope club secretary by yourself and find out whatever you can. No problem, is there?'

'I'll go this afternoon,' said Sarah.

'Right,' said Graham, 'that's all settled. Let's go off and start work on the Skipper's project. I'll get the equipment.'

He jumped up and was about to go through into the other room when he suddenly paused and looked at Sarah.

'You won't tell anybody about the equipment we're using – and where we're using it, will you?' he said, a little suspiciously.

'Of course she won't, Graham,' said Tom.

'The Skipper did say to keep it a secret from everybody but the three of us,' Graham retorted, sternly. Nevertheless, he disappeared and returned a moment later with a canvas bag which seemed to contain some heavy objects, and an instrument which Sarah recognised as a metal detector.

They all left HQ together and Tom locked up. 'I'll just show Sarah where we keep the key,' he said as the others made for their bikes, and led her to the crumbling old wall which had once surrounded the garden. He took out a loose brick revealing a cavity behind it.

'Don't mind Graham,' he said with a grin as he put the key in. 'He'll come round. And as for this business of the other project ... well ... I'm sorry we've got to make such a mystery of it, but Graham is right. We did promise the Skipper and a promise is a promise.'

He reflected for a moment.

'Still, there's no harm in telling you who the Skipper is. He's the coach at Madford Rowing Club. One of Graham's heroes. Graham makes heroes out of people – usually they're dead fighter pilots killed in action and so on – but the Skipper's a real live one to Graham, and he worships the ground he walks on –'

53

'Tom – time's getting on!' came a yell from Graham.

Tom bent down and plucked a stem of red clover.

'Welcome to the Clover Club,' he said, presenting it to Sarah. 'May it help to bring colour, romance and adventure into your life.'

'It already has,' said Sarah, smiling.

She waved to the three boys as they set off, the equipment tied to the luggage racks of Graham's and Rodge's bikes.

'See you tomorrow!' yelled Rodge cheerfully.

'Oh, and Sarah,' called Tom, 'you'll bring the book of Edmund Cope's poems, won't you. I want to read them.' If he noticed the way Graham winced, he didn't let on.

When they'd gone, Sarah didn't hurry to set off herself. She sat on the saddle of her bike reflecting what a sense of excitement she felt at having become a member of the Clover Club, even a temporary Grade-Two member. If only Graham didn't so obviously object to her ...

And then, over near the wall, she noticed a tap on a stand-pipe. Going over to it she turned it on and was rewarded by the sight of a stream of water emerging from it, rust-coloured at first then becoming clearer. It was working! And she had a clean cloth in her saddlebag! She went over and got it and held it under the tap. She'd been just longing to clean those windows.

'Maybe I am only a temporary member but I'm going to make a few changes around this HQ,' she thought with satisfaction.

Just after four that afternoon, Sarah got off the 'bus in Hamblesey, Edmund Cope's poems in her hand, and looked at the piece of paper the librarian had given her.

'Mr Peter Warden, 19, Duckbury,' it read.

Duckbury was a narrow, quaint little street of terraced houses near the river. As she approached number 19, the door opened and a stream of people, about a dozen in all, started to emerge. They were being seen off by an eager young man in a thin white summer sweater and carrying a pair of horn-rimmed spectacles which he waved about

54

enthusiastically as he spoke a word or two to each departing guest.

'A meeting of the Edmund Cope society, I suppose,' thought Sarah as she paused to watch them, fascinated by the thought that they had all gathered to talk about that remote figure who had carved his initials, and Miss Maybury's, on the tree.

'Excuse me,' she said, as the young man was about to close the door after the last guest had emerged, 'are you Mr Warden?'

'That's right.'

'Cherringham Library gave me your name. They said –'

'Have you come to join the society?' he said eagerly. 'Come in.'

He led her through the entrance hall into a sort of study, or maybe it was a dining room. A room almost filled by a long table with chairs around it. The walls were lined with bookshelves and there was a very old gramophone in one corner. It was astonishingly untidy with papers and books strewn everywhere.

'Take a seat and I'll tell you about it,' he said.

'Well, I haven't actually come here to join the society,' said Sarah hastily. 'It's just that I want to find out something about Edmund Cope for a – a project.'

Sarah had pondered about what to say. She'd decided against telling him about her visit to Miss Maybury because – who could tell? – it might give eager beavers from the society the idea of visiting Lockets themselves and that would be the last thing Miss Maybury would want.

'School English project, I suppose,' said Mr Warden. He flung himself into a chair and put his feet on the table. He didn't seem in the least disappointed. 'Well, fire away. Ask me anything you want.'

'I – I just want to know about the part of his life when he lived in this area.'

'Ah,' said Mr Warden, 'you've asked me a question I could take two days to reply to, talking non-stop. I'll try to cut it down to half an hour.'

He became dreamy, gazing out of the window as if he'd forgotten she was there.

'You see there's a mystery surrounding the time when he lived around here, a very romantic mystery. He came to this area in 1913 and rented a tiny cottage by the river because he wanted to get away from London to the peace and quiet of the country. Somewhere near the river where he could row for relaxation because he loved boats.

'And it was while he was living in this cottage that his poetry took off. Up till then it had been nice, very pleasant ... suddenly it became inspired. And it's obvious that somebody inspired him. He makes mysterious references in his poems to somebody whom he loved very dearly – here, give me that book you're holding and I'll read some of the poems to show you what I mean. The mystery is, you see, who *was* the person who inspired him and turned him into a great poet?'

Sarah handed the book over.

'So nobody knows,' thought Sarah. 'I think I know who it was. It was Miss Maybury who inspired him. Miss Maybury, the batty old lady of Lockets who's living like a hermit and fell over the other day and couldn't get up herself. She was very lovely and they used to meet in a glade – secretly, maybe – and carve hearts on a tree – and now she's batty and thinks he's going to come back to her ...'

Mr Warden was talking on, reading the poems to her, telling her how Edmund Cope had joined the army in 1914 after the first world war had broken out and had been killed in action. His war poems, full of nostalgia and dreams of home, had also had references to this mysterious person.

'Are you listening?' he asked her suddenly. 'You look as if you're dreaming.'

'Oh, I'm listening, all right,' said Sarah, softly, 'yes, I'm listening very hard ...'

'Yes, I see what he means,' said Tom. 'Edmund Cope was talking to somebody in some of these poems, wasn't he?

Somebody he was really crazy about. And it was old Miss Maybury, we think! Incredible, isn't it?'

It was just after three o'clock the following day and Sarah had met up with Tom, Graham and Rodge at the private road sign. Tom was sitting on a nearby gate reading Edmund Cope's poems. He'd insisted on doing so straight away after Sarah had reported what she'd found out.

Graham and Rodge were prowling about restlessly, waiting for him.

'Did you finish off your job for the – er – for the Skipper, yesterday?' Sarah asked them.

'No,' said Rodge with a rueful grin. 'Didn't find a thing. Pity because the Skipper's promised the club a new boat if we find –'

He stopped, realising that Graham was shooting him a warning glance. 'Sorry,' he said, still grinning, 'that's careless talk, isn't it. I'm already finding it hard to remember this stuff about you only being a temporary member, Sarah.'

Sarah warmed to him even more than she had already, especially as she saw the way Graham was scowling. But she was surprised by what he'd just said, too. A new boat? Whatever they were doing must be pretty important to the Skipper.

'This cottage that Edmund Cope stayed in,' said Tom, looking up from the book again, 'where was it?'

'It's disappeared now,' said Sarah, 'pulled down or fallen down. But it was called Willow Cottage and it was on the river somewhere between Lockets and Hamblesey.'

'Oh, come on,' said Graham. 'If we're going to Lockets then let's go instead of sitting around reading poetry.'

'Got to do our homework first,' said Tom, cheerfully. 'Who knows – the key to this whole baffling mystery of what a long-dead poet is doing wandering around Lockets may be somewhere in these poems.'

'Anyway,' he said to Graham, 'I'd have thought you might be a little bit interested in some of these poems about the Great War.'

57

'You can keep the poets,' said Graham. 'It's the men of action I'm interested in. Like the Mad Major of Saint Martin who attacked ten enemy planes single-handed so as to keep them from attacking his airfield before it was ready – but Edmund Cope was just a glamour-boy wasn't he.'

He glared at Sarah as if it were her fault.

Graham wasn't missing a chance to take a dig at her. It was as if he were reminding her all the time that she mustn't get any ideas above her station.

'Come on,' said Tom, jumping off the gate and handing the book back to Sarah. 'Let's go to Lockets then. I'll finish that off later.'

As they walked in through the gates and along the curving drive, Sarah again had the feeling that the past was closing in around her; a golden past that was more beautiful, romantic and mysterious than the world of the present outside the gates. Glancing at the boys, she thought that they, too, seemed affected by the atmosphere; even Graham, for all his words.

It was very hot. Sarah remembered reading somewhere that the summer of 1914 had been long and golden and this summer was now getting the same feeling about it ...

'Do you really think she'll let us in?' asked Rodge doubtfully, as they stood before the front porch.

'We shall see,' said Tom. He walked up the steps and wielded the great knocker.

This time there was no waiting before they heard the tap of Miss Maybury's stick. It sounded brisk and eager. The flap of the letter-box opened.

'Who is that?' came Miss Maybury's voice, a little tremulous this time.

Sarah stepped forward.

'It's Sarah Brownbridge. You remember – I said I'd like to come back with some friends.'

The flap clicked shut, the key turned heavily and the door opened.

'I've been hoping you'd come back,' said Miss Maybury.

8

In the Footsteps of the Ghost

Miss Maybury seemed to be in a state of suppressed excitement.

'You don't mind my bringing my friends with me, do you?' asked Sarah, a little anxious, stepping aside so that the old lady could see the boys.

Miss Maybury's face clouded over for a moment. 'Friends?' she said doubtfully. 'Oh, I hadn't realised –'

'I'll need them if I'm to look upstairs. You remember I promised to do that.'

Miss Maybury reflected for a moment. Then she smiled as if she were doing something very daring.

'Very well,' she said. 'Since they're *your* friends.'

'Hallo, Miss Maybury,' said Tom, cheerfully, as they came close up to the door. 'You've met me before, anyway.'

It was amazing to see them all entering Lockets, somehow: two different ages coming together. Rodge looked about him wonderingly. Graham had his scowl on.

'Has this – this person been back again?' said Tom as soon as he'd introduced them.

'Yes,' said the old lady, almost whispering. 'He came again –'

'Then should we go straight upstairs and see if we can see anything – ?' asked Sarah.

Miss Maybury looked at Sarah. She still had that air of nervous, suppressed excitement about her.

'Before you do that, I'd like to see you by yourself. I have something to show you.'

Sarah glanced at Tom. 'We'll wait here,' he said.

Sarah followed Miss Maybury into the dining room. 'How slim and straight she is!' she thought. 'Even now when she's very old. This is the person who inspired Edmund Cope. Edmund Cope who was just a remote romantic name to me till I came here – but was famous in his day!'

Miss Maybury went over to the dresser and opened a drawer. She seemed very excited, like someone who has been given a present and is dying to show it off.

'You see,' she said, 'when he came – it was the evening before last – I heard him and I went to the foot of the stairs to call him and then – then something fell. This. It belonged to a – a friend of mine.'

She turned round and Sarah saw that she had tears in her eyes. She was holding a man's handkerchief. The initials E.C. were embroidered in one corner.

'Edmund Cope's handkerchief!' thought Sarah, astounded. Then she had doubts. Handkerchiefs with initials on them were surely easy to come by –

'I know it's his not simply because the initials are his but because I embroidered them myself,' said Miss Maybury. 'I embroidered several of them in the same blue letters.'

She turned and put it back in the drawer.

'I wanted so much to show it to someone,' she said, and Sarah realised that her tears were of joy.

'Miss Maybury,' Sarah said nervously to her back, 'you think it's this friend – this friend with the initials E.C. – who's coming into the house, don't you.'

'Now I know it is,' said the old lady.

'That makes life difficult,' said Tom a few moments later.

Sarah had left Miss Maybury in the dining room and joined the boys in the hall.

'All she wants us to go looking round upstairs for is to find some more proof that it's Edmund Cope who's walking around. She wouldn't want to hear anything different.'

'She really is batty,' said Graham.

'But Edmund Cope's handkerchief – how did it get there?' said Sarah.

Tom shrugged. 'Perhaps she's confusing it with a hand-

kerchief she embroidered. I suppose if you want to believe
something badly enough, you'll convince yourself of anything.'

'I suppose so,' said Sarah, 'but ... but ... what puzzles
me is why anybody should want to keep on coming back
to Lockets and walking around. What point would there
be in it?'

'Let's go up and see if we can find out,' said Tom.

He led the way up the stairs.

'Crikey!' he said at the top as he came in sight of the
view that had sent Sarah rapidly downstairs again on their
previous visit. 'Cobwebby, isn't it! Hope you don't mind
spiders?' he said to Sarah.

'Not so much now I've got company,' she said. 'But it's
still pretty creepy, isn't it?'

They moved forward along the corridor.

'Somebody has been up here, you know,' said Rodge
suddenly. 'Look!'

He paused by one of the doors that led off the corridor
and then glanced round at some of the others.

'The cobwebs have broken away from all the doors.'

'You're right,' said Tom, exploring further along. 'From
every single one!' He looked at Sarah. 'Then somebody
definitely has been up here lately. That wasn't imagination.'

'Thank you!' said Sarah demurely.

'But surely ghosts don't open doors,' said Graham. 'They
go through them.'

'I dunno,' said Tom. 'I'm not an expert on ghosts. Not
yet, anyway. Let's open a few doors ourselves.'

They opened one at random. A huge bedroom, airless
and smelling of damp, with a great mahogany bed in one
corner; browning portraits round the walls; a jug and
basin on a marble washstand; a great family Bible on a
bedside table –

'Somebody has been in here. Definitely!' said Sarah.
'Look at the bible. It's been moved.'

Beside the Bible was a shining, dust-free oblong where it

had lain till very recently.

'Why should anyone come into the house and move a bible?' said Tom.

'Ghosts don't move things either,' said Graham.

'I don't see why they shouldn't,' said Rodge, looking about, a little nervously Sarah thought. 'Poltergeists throw things so why shouldn't ghosts just move things.'

'Let's see if we can spot how he gets in,' said Tom. 'Where did you see him climb up the ivy, Sarah?'

'Back of the house, on the right as you come up from the river.'

'That should be the last door on the right. Let's see what room that is.'

It was a huge Victorian study, or library, of the sort that Sarah had only seen in pictures. Bookshelves lined the walls. There must have been thousands of books there, all beautifully bound. A vast leather topped desk stood in the centre of the room and in the corner was an ornate antique library table with a globe of the world on it. The mantelpiece was crowded with brass and china ornaments. It all looked very complete as if someone had walked out of the room intending to return within a few minutes and had never come back.

However, it was the windows that attracted their attention at first. They were french windows giving on to a balcony. Tom went over to them, turned the handle and pushed them open. He stepped out on to the balcony.

'Couldn't be easier, could it?' he said, as they all followed him.

They peered together over the balustrade.

'Look – just climbs up the ivy, over here, through the doors ...'

'But what for?' said Sarah. From the balcony she could see the river gliding slowly along between the willows, and the top of the big willow where she herself had sat. It was so easy to imagine that the mysterious intruder *was* Edmund Cope. Perhaps it was ...

'Have you noticed that nothing seems to have been taken from this room?' asked Tom, stepping back inside again, 'although a lot of these ornaments look pretty valuable.'

'And the books,' said Rodge. 'Just look at them. They must be worth a small fortune by themselves.'

'So whoever he is, he's not a burglar,' said Tom, helplessly. 'Anyway what burglar would be carrying around handkerchiefs with E.C. on them? *Why* is he coming, whoever he is? And why'd he drop that handkerchief?'

Rodge took out a book from one of the shelves. 'But there's no dust on this book,' he said, 'in fact there isn't any on any of them.'

'No more there is!' said Tom as he and Graham peered along the shelves. 'They've been dusted – every single one!'

'The ornaments on the mantelpiece have been moved, too,' said Sarah.

They all looked at each other.

'Maybe he's searching for something,' said Sarah.

'Looking behind books, inside vases ... ? Might be,' said Tom.

'What else could it be?' said Graham, who seemed to be getting steadily more interested and forgetting to look slightly bored by the whole thing. 'But what would he be looking for?'

'And has he found it?' said Sarah.

'Look,' said Tom, 'there's only one way we're going to find out. We've got to keep watch. Lie in wait for him, see what he does, then follow him. We know how he gets in now so it shouldn't be difficult.'

'You mean – hide here? In these rooms after dark?' said Sarah with a shudder.

'We'll have to work that out. Now we're sure of his movements it'll be simple enough. Let's have a look around the rest of the upstairs to see if we can spot anything else.'

In each bedroom they went into there were signs that someone had been before them recently.

'If he is looking for something he's looking for it pretty thoroughly,' said Tom, puzzled.

'I wonder how many people used to live here?' Graham

63

mused. 'There are a lot of bedrooms and you could put the whole of the upstairs of our house into one of them.'

'Guest bedrooms, I suppose,' said Tom.

There was another suite of much smaller bedrooms at the top of a further flight of narrow, winding stairs. Tom said they must have been for the servants. There were signs that those, too, had been entered.

Then, just before going downstairs again, they went into the last of the main bedrooms.

It was different from the others. They had all been stern, rather spartan looking. This one managed to be pretty, despite dust and cobwebs, with its chintzy curtains and chair cover. It looked like the bedroom of a young girl.

'Surely this was Miss Maybury's room,' said Sarah.

There was a large Victorian wardrobe in the corner and as the boys started to wander around the room looking for more signs, Sarah went over to it and opened the door.

'Oh, look!' she cried in sudden excitement.

She hadn't really expected that there would still be clothes in it. But there were. A whole row of dresses.

'Miss Maybury's clothes from when she was a young girl!'

The boys looked round but they weren't very interested. 'Should we go back downstairs now?' suggested Rodge. 'We've seen everything.'

'Wait – wait!' said Sarah. She had been flicking through the dresses but had suddenly stopped, gazing at one of them. She took it from the wardrobe and laid it on the bed. Then, excitedly, she started to take the envelope containing the pictures out of her pocket.

'I think this is the dress she was wearing!'

'Wearing when?' said Rodge, puzzled. 'What are you talking about?'

'In the picture! At the garden party!'

She stared at the picture.

'Yes, it was,' she whispered, 'there's no doubt about it.'

She picked up the dress and put it over her arm, running the fingers of her other hand over it. Somehow, more

64

than anything else, it brought that golden day in 1914 right here into the present. To be touching it, holding it!

'Let me see,' said Tom, taking the picture from her. He seemed impressed by it, too.

'Oh, come on,' snorted Graham.

Sarah took the picture back from Tom and replaced it in the envelope, then put it back in her pocket.

'I'm going to show the dress to Miss Maybury,' she announced.

'Why?' asked Rodge.

'Because I have the feeling she might want to see it. And anyway I want to show it to her.'

'Why not?' said Tom. 'It might bring back some memories.' He seemed to understand.

Sarah led the way down the stairs with the dress still over her arm. It was a relief to be leaving the cobwebs and the dust and the smell of damp.

Miss Maybury was standing in the hall, waiting for them eagerly.

'Did you find anything?' she asked, as Sarah joined her.

'We found signs that somebody's been up there, Miss Maybury. Somebody who's been moving about, disturbing things ... and we found out how he got in.'

'But ... but nothing else? Nothing at all ... ?'

The old lady's face showed bitter disappointment and Sarah wondered what she'd been hoping for. Probably she didn't know herself. She'd just been hoping for *something*, anything ... maybe she'd hoped they'd find Edmund Cope himself.

'Miss Maybury,' she said, 'I hope you don't mind but – do you remember this?'

She held the dress up against herself. She knew at once that the old lady did remember it from the way her face changed and her hand tightened on her stick. Sarah could almost see how the dress was making memories come flooding back.

'Yes, I remember it!' murmured Miss Maybury. She was in a world of her own.

Deciding that it was best to strike while the iron was

65

hot, Sarah started to take the pictures from her pocket with the intention of showing them to the old lady. But she was forestalled.

'I know,' said Miss Maybury, timidly, 'that you're going to think I'm a very foolish old woman, but I wonder – I wonder if you would do something for me?'

'Well, yes, anything,' said Sarah anxiously. 'What is it you want?'

'I wonder if you'd put it on?'

9

Miss Maybury's Story

'I'd love to!' said Sarah, astonished. She glanced round at
the boys who were staring at Miss Maybury.

'Batty!' muttered Graham.

'I think it will fit you very well,' said Miss Maybury,
'although I was some years older than you when I wore it.
I'll show you where you can change.'

'See you in a minute,' Sarah said to the boys, about to
follow the old lady along the hall.

'I knew she was taken by you,' whispered Tom. 'She's
seeing you as herself – as she used to be when she was a
girl.'

'I suppose so,' Sarah whispered back. 'She's pretending
all the time, isn't she? She never stops living in the past.'

'We'll be exploring the grounds while you're doing that,'
said Tom in a normal voice as Miss Maybury paused and
glanced back, waiting for Sarah. 'Come on, you two.'

Sarah followed the old lady along a corridor that left
the hall at right angles. 'This is the room I use for sleeping
in now,' said Miss Maybury, opening a door for her. 'I
shall be in the dining room.'

The room Sarah was in was large and had once been a
sitting room, too. Or drawing room, perhaps. Now, in
addition to its other furnishings there was a bed and a
dressing table with mirror.

They had passed several other doors on their way there
and Sarah idly wondered what lay behind them and why
the mysterious visitor always went upstairs.

She stood in front of the mirror feeling vaguely silly.
Dressing up to please Miss Maybury, indeed!

And yet, as she looked at the dress ... and yet ...

Why should she keep on denying it to herself? Deep

down, she'd been dying to try on that dress from the moment she'd seen it. If Miss Maybury wanted to indulge in day-dreams, so did she. To be as that girl in the pictures, in the misty past ...

'Miss Maybury,' she said softly a few minutes later as she entered the dining room.

The old lady was sitting in her chair by the windows which were slightly open, the sunlight streaming in. She turned her head.

'Me ... as I was,' she whispered.

'I'm not beautiful like you were,' said Sarah, but Miss Maybury didn't seem to hear.

'I know this must seem very foolish to you,' she said, 'but I'm an old woman and memories are all I have to live for. Memories, and hope.

'Besides, the dress suits you. You have such a sweet face, an old-fashioned face.'

Through the french windows, Sarah could see the boys. They were investigating down by the river, looking at the landing stage and the boathouse. She had a sudden desire to go out on the lawns where the garden party had been held.

'Miss Maybury,' she said, 'may I go out into the garden like this?'

'Of course,' said Miss Maybury. She rose from her chair. 'I'd like you to put this on, too.' She went over to the table and for the first time Sarah saw that she had a hat waiting for her there, an enormous wide-brimmed hat. She picked it up and placed it on Sarah's head.

'There,' she said.

Sarah pushed open the french windows and stepped out on to the terrace. Then, descending the few steps, started to walk down the lawns towards the river. She felt intensely romantic.

It was very warm. The boys seemed to have disappeared and there was no sound but the little noises of birds amongst the trees. Then ahead of her she saw the fountain and she had a sudden whim.

Glancing round she saw that Miss Maybury was sitting

down again, watching her, no doubt living again those days in 1914 when she had been a young girl. Sarah turned back to face the river again and then, picking up her long skirt a little with one hand, she started to run. The exhilaration of it! To run just as Miss Maybury had all those years ago just before the camera had caught her!

It happened by chance. She was just by the fountain when Tom scrambled on to the landing stage, apparently from some boat which was now moored to it. As he saw her, he looked startled, then smiled and waved, and she halted, waving back at him joyously. She was on exactly the same spot where Miss Maybury had been when the camera had caught her.

Turning, Sarah walked back up the lawn again, crossed the terrace and re-entered the dining room. Miss Maybury was standing up now. She seemed to be trembling. Sarah's little bit of play-acting had struck home.

'Did that remind you of something?' asked Sarah, innocently.

'H – how did you know that?' said Miss Maybury. She was still trembling.

'I'll show you,' said Sarah. 'I won't be a minute.'

She hurried back to the room where she had left her own clothes and returned a few minutes later with the pictures. Miss Maybury was seated again and she put them into her hand, the one showing her as a young girl on top.

'I bought these pictures in Cherringham market,' she said softly. 'Do you recognise them? Do you remember when they were taken?'

Miss Maybury looked through them slowly, as if mesmerised.

'Of course I recognise the occasion,' she said, and her face was furrowed with lines of anguish, 'how could I ever forget?'

'Miss Maybury, when I stopped by the fountain just now, I saw Tom. Tell me if I'm being nosy but when *you* stopped, what was it *you* saw? What made you look so happy? Was it – ?'

'It was Edmund,' said Miss Maybury. 'Edmund Cope.'

She'd turned her head so that Sarah couldn't see her face. She was speaking almost to herself, remembering, seeing it all again in her mind.

'He'd just rowed to the landing-stage and jumped up on it. He was smiling at me and waving. It was the happiest moment – the happiest day – of my life. That's one reason I can't ever forget it.'

'And the other reason is – the other reason is ...'

Her voice seemed to dissolve into nothing and Sarah realised that she was incapable of going on.

Sarah dropped to her knees beside the chair. Looking up, she could see part of the old lady's face, even though it was turned away from her, lined but still firm, still beautiful.

'Miss Maybury,' she said, 'won't you tell me what the other reason is? And why you live here all by yourself like this in a house that you keep just as it was in 1914? And – and why you're so sure that it's Edmund Cope who's coming into the house and ... oh, Miss Maybury, wouldn't you like to tell somebody, even if it is only me?'

And suddenly Miss Maybury started to talk, quietly, almost in a murmur, but without hesitating. It was as if she had been waiting all those years for a chance to tell somebody.

She had met Edmund Cope in the spring of 1914 when she had been a young girl, living at Lockets with her parents and a staff of servants.

He was already well-known, partly because of his poetry, and partly because of his charm and dazzling good looks. When he came to live in the area for a while, he was invited to every party for miles.

She met him at a house party where she had gone with her parents. She had watched, fascinated, as he entered, the centre of attention, fussed over by everyone. She hadn't dreamed that he would even speak to her.

To her amazement, he had walked over to her and introduced himself, just as if he were someone she could never have heard of.

'By the end of the evening,' said Miss Maybury, 'it was as if I had known him forever. I was in love with him and I thought he was in love with me. We were sweethearts.'

Sarah had never heard the word 'sweetheart' used sincerely and naturally like that. But coming from Miss Maybury it didn't sound silly, not silly at all.

That evening had changed Miss Maybury's life. During the summer of 1914 she and Edmund Cope had spent every moment they could together. It had become a golden, magical, enchanted summer. They had picnicked and punted and ridden their bicycles. And they had found a beautiful, secret little dell in the woods along the river, where he'd read his poems to her as he'd composed them. It had become their own special dell.

'Many of the poems were written to me,' said Miss Maybury, 'to me alone. He said that he was writing better poetry because of me.'

'I knew it,' Sarah murmured to herself.

But her parents had not been so happy about Edmund Cope. They had not been strict parents – far from it. They had allowed her to see him as often as she wanted, probably hoping it would end more quickly that way. But they had never stopped warning her against him.

'You're a silly girl, he'll break your heart,' her father told her often, 'just as he's already broken the hearts of a dozen other girls. When he tires of his country cottage, he'll tire of you, too, and simply disappear.'

'He won't!' she had told them, laughing. 'He won't, he won't, he won't.'

In spite of her pleadings, they had never invited him into the house. They refused to show friendship towards him themselves. It was as if they had made up their minds for certain that one day he would behave badly towards their daughter ...

Until the garden party; the garden party shown in the photographs. It was to be held on her birthday and at last, worn down by her pleadings, her parents relented. He was invited and he came.

He arrived in a rowing boat as he always did when he came to the house to call for her, tying up to the landing-stage and jumping ashore. As always, wherever he went, he'd immediately been the centre of attention. But he'd never left her side. He'd chatted to her parents and seemed to get on well. It had been an afternoon of such happiness. But much more was to come.

Before leaving he had drawn her aside and told her that he would be going to London the following day to make arrangements about publishing some of his poems. He would be away for a week but when he came back he wanted to meet her in their dell. And then he would want her to take him to the house to meet her father again. Because he felt now that the ice was broken and her parents had shown some friendliness towards him, he'd be able to ask permission to marry her. If she wanted that ...

She had stood on the landing-stage waving to him as he rowed away, smiling, between the green, whispering willows, until he disappeared from sight round the bend in the river. She had spent a week of delicious tormented bliss waiting for him to come back, longing to tell her parents just how wrong they'd been, but knowing she mustn't. And then she had set off for the dell to wait for him, running through the woods for sheer joy and happiness.

He didn't come. She never saw him again.

Soon after that, war was declared. Her father told her that he'd heard that Edmund Cope had joined the army.

'He had to let you down sooner or later,' her father had growled. 'It's better that you find out sooner.'

Some long time later his name had appeared in the casualty lists. He had transferred to the Royal Flying Corps. He was missing, presumed dead.

As the years had gone by, Miss Maybury's parents had died and the servants had gone away, leaving her alone.

'Then he did let you down,' said Sarah, sadly. 'He didn't love you, after all.'

Miss Maybury rose and, leaning on her stick, gazed out

of the window. Tom was coming up the lawns but she didn't seem to see him.

'Oh, but he did love me. He still does.'

'But —'

'Why didn't he come? I don't know, but there must have been a reason. One day he'll come back and tell me what it was. All I know is that I couldn't have been wrong about him.'

Miss Maybury's voice was dropping lower and lower. She was murmuring as if to herself.

'When I was left by myself, I rearranged the house. I made it just as it was in the summer of 1914. Because this way I can look out of the window and I can believe that at any moment I'll see him appearing over the landing-stage as he climbs out of his boat. And he'll wave to me and come walking up the lawns to tell me why he never came to our meeting ...'

She turned to look at Sarah.

'You're thinking my father was right, aren't you? I was a silly, romantic girl and now ... now I've only to look in a mirror to see that —'

She turned her head away sharply and sat down again.

'It doesn't matter what I see in a mirror. There are more important things than that.'

Sarah got up and, almost without thinking, put an arm round Miss Maybury's shoulders. Then she withdrew it.

'I'll go and change into my own clothes again, shall I?'

Miss Maybury nodded. She had gone into a reverie. Her mind was still in 1914.

Sarah quietly left the room. Tom was just coming up the hall, grinning and admiring the clothes.

'You look fabulous,' he said. 'You made my hair stand on end when I saw you coming down the lawn. I thought I really had stepped back into the past.'

She did a gracious little twirl for him. But it was an absent-minded one. Her mind was still in 1914, too.

'What were you doing at the landing-stage?' she asked him.

'We've found a boat that's not altogether rotten and

73

still floats, so we had a little row in it. Come and see it.'

'All right. As soon as I've changed. I've got a lot to report.'

'Good. We've got to have a meeting anyway to decide what to do next. That's why I came to fetch you. There's a little bit of disagreement going on.'

'Oh dear! With Graham?'

'You've guessed it.'

That brought Sarah firmly back into the present.

'I'll be with you in a couple of minutes.'

10

The Clover Club Lies in Wait

It felt peculiar to be back in her own clothes as she hurried down the lawns a few minutes later. Maybe they were easier to move about in, but she didn't feel graceful or romantic as she had done in Miss Maybury's.

The boys were sitting in a rowing boat, Tom holding it against the landing-stage with one hand while Rodge held the oars. Graham was looking martyred.

'Squeeze in and we'll have a little row first before we put it back in the boathouse,' said Tom.

Sarah stepped down and sat beside Tom. There was water slopping about in the bottom of the boat but it seemed solid enough.

'Nice, isn't it,' said Tom, contentedly, as Rodge pulled out into the river. 'You can see why Graham and Rodge are so keen on rowing.'

Graham's stubborn look didn't flicker.

Sarah was looking at the house, seeing it now as she'd seen it the first time but with new eyes, knowing now that that lonely figure was sitting at the window watching and waiting as she had watched and waited for – for how many years?

'All right,' said Tom. 'I suppose this is as good a place to report as any. Make your report, agent number four.'

Sarah told them what Miss Maybury had said to her.

'Does she *really* believe he's going to come back to her?' asked Rodge, sceptically, when she'd finished.

Sarah hesitated. 'I – I think she *wants* to believe it. It makes her happy to believe it, so she does.'

'And what happens,' said Tom slowly, 'if we prove to her that this person who's coming into the house isn't Edmund Cope at all? When she so badly wants it to be?'

'I've been wondering the same thing,' said Sarah. 'We don't want to break her heart and yet – well, we do have to find out, don't we, because heaven knows what he's up to!'

'Anyway,' said Tom thoughtfully, 'perhaps it is Edmund Cope.'

'Oh, don't be silly, Tom,' said Rodge. 'I didn't expect you of all people to sound as if you believe in ghosts.'

'Well,' said Tom, 'if you can think of any other reason why somebody in Edwardian clothes should be wandering around Lockets at night without taking anything – *and* dropping handkerchiefs to Miss Maybury – just let me know. In the meantime . . .'

Sarah stared at him. She had allowed similar thoughts to run through her own mind but she wouldn't have dared to say them out loud. To hear Tom, of all people, made her shiver slightly.

'. . . we'd better make a decision on what we were talking about before,' continued Tom, 'that is, when we set our trap for this ghost. What does Sarah think?'

'Soon as possible as far as I'm concerned,' said Sarah promptly. 'Tonight. We could all go home now and have some tea and be back before it gets dark.'

'Exactly what I thought,' said Tom.

'I think we should get back to the Skipper's job for the rest of today,' said Graham, stubbornly. 'You know he's told us it's urgent and we've done nothing today.'

So that was what the disagreement had been about! Graham was back on his hobby-horse about the Skipper.

'Oh well,' said Sarah, 'if Graham really feels that –'

'No,' said Tom, firmly. 'Graham's entitled to his opinion but we've got to settle this properly. The Skipper's job probably is urgent but I think this is even more so. Somebody's getting into a house where there's an old lady living alone. He hasn't done anything yet but you never know – tonight may be the night he does. I don't think we've been treating this urgently enough and I think it's about time we started.'

'If we really think he may do anything to Miss Maybury,

then we should tell the police,' said Graham, still stubborn.

'We can't,' said Tom. 'We promised.' He looked around. 'So is everybody ready to take a vote on it now we're all here? Who's in favour of laying the trap tonight?'

He and Rodge raised their hands.

'Against?'

'I'm abstaining,' said Sarah, as Graham raised his. She felt much too new a member of the Clover Club to be anything but neutral, however strongly she felt.

'Carried,' said Tom, 'and it's no use complaining, Graham. You know the rules.'

'I'm not complaining,' said Graham, but his face was set.

Sarah was relieved the vote had gone the way it had. Nevertheless she hated these disagreements and the feeling that she was coming between the boys. It was obvious that Graham hadn't really accepted her.

'Graham isn't usually like this,' Rodge whispered to her a few minutes later as they put the boat away in its boathouse, among the half-submerged punts that lay there.

'No, I'm sure he isn't,' Sarah whispered back a little unhappily.

She knew Rodge meant well but it made her feel worse to be reminded that Graham's disagreeableness was all her fault.

They made their plans sitting on the grass by the landing-stage in the sunshine. It was agreed that the object would be to lie in wait for whoever it was who was entering the house, try to see what he was doing in there and then follow him when he left – and find out where he went. It would all have to be done very quietly so as not to alert him.

'We know precisely what route he takes, so there won't be any difficulty seeing him go in and out. I should think two of us hiding outside and two of us upstairs in the house would be best. Where would you rather be, Sarah?'

'Outside,' said Sarah, at once.

'Better take up positions early because we know he arrives straight after dusk and we don't want him to see us.'

'What about Miss Maybury?' said Rodge. 'Do we tell her what we're doing?'

Tom considered. 'I don't think so,' he said. He looked at Sarah questioningly. She shook her head.

'I don't think so either. I'm not honestly quite sure how she'd behave. And besides ...' she hesitated. 'I think it would be better to find out who or what it is ourselves first, before we decide what we're going to say to her.'

'My feelings exactly,' said Tom. 'We'll do this one by stealth.'

Ten minutes later, having told Miss Maybury they were going but that they would see her again very soon, they were on their bikes to their various homes.

'Hallo, stranger,' said Sarah's mother. 'Popped in for a meal?'

'It's nice to see you, too,' said Sarah, 'though I do have to go out again soon, as it happens. Got some secret business on with the Clover Club.'

Mrs Brownbridge put on her look of tolerant disbelief. Sarah had known she wouldn't believe a word of it, which was why she'd been able to say it so casually.

'Well, it's nice to be out in the open air with your new friends,' she said, rather patronisingly, thought Sarah, 'especially in weather like this. It's just getting hotter and hotter.'

After tea, Sarah wondered about ringing up Gillian to tell her what she was missing, but decided against it. She wandered around restlessly for a time, unable to settle. She couldn't get the story Miss Maybury had told her out of her mind.

'Why didn't Edmund Cope come back to that meeting?' she wondered. 'Why did he just disappear? *Why?*'

She was pleased to see that the curtains were up and hanging straight. Her father was watering the garden and she went out to help him.

As soon as she'd finished, she set off back to Lockets early and waited for the boys by the private road sign. She was keyed up and excited by the thought of what they were going to do. She didn't feel at all afraid, not when the boys were going to be with her.

Tom and Rodge arrived together and Graham a minute or two later.

'Everybody remembered torches?' asked Tom. They all had.

'Do you know any Morse code?' he said to Sarah.

'None,' she said.

'Didn't think you would. No matter. Graham does.'

'So when should we take up positions?' asked Rodge.

'No point in hurrying. We know he doesn't go in the house till after dark and she's turned the lights on. And we don't want to risk being seen by Miss Maybury. He probably comes round to the shrubbery at dusk.'

They waited till the shadows had lengthened and the warmth was going out of the air before moving in through the gates of Lockets. Keeping to the shelter of the trees, just in case Miss Maybury should be looking out of any of the front windows, they passed across the front of the house and then made their way down the far side to the corner where the library balcony was.

'He came out of the shrubbery, there,' said Sarah, nodding towards it.

'Perhaps Rodge and I had better take the inside positions,' said Tom. 'Graham and Sarah outside.'

'Sooner you than me,' said Sarah, with a little shudder. 'How are you going to get upstairs?'

'Same way that Edmund Cope does. Up the ivy and through the balcony window. Let's find good hiding places for you two first though.'

Sarah wondered if Tom were trying to establish some feeling of comradeship between her and Graham by leaving them out here together. Certainly Graham seemed to be forgetting his sullenness now as he got caught up in the excitement.

Tom moved quietly in amongst the shrubs and the others followed. The shrubbery was now little more than a jungle and there were plenty of hiding places.

'Here's a good one for you, Sarah,' said Tom, lifting some branches which swept down to the ground. 'You'll be invisible if you kneel down behind these.'

Sarah crawled into the dark interior of an evergreen shrub. The leaves smelled sweetly as she brushed against them.

'Can you see out all right?'

'Perfect. I can see the balcony from here.'

'Fine. If you're lucky he might pass close enough for you to get a good look at him. The main thing is to watch when he comes out and then follow him and find out where he goes.

'If it's to a car, get the make and colour and number. If it's to a bike, keep on following him on yours. And remember that Graham and maybe Rodge and me could be following as well, so don't get in anybody's way.'

He grinned.

'That's all assuming he comes tonight. He might not.'

He looked round briskly.

'We're off now. Make sure you see where Graham hides so that you can work together if you have to.'

He moved away and Sarah watched as Graham concealed himself in another shrub. If Edmund Cope repeated his movements of the other evening, she estimated that he would probably pass right between them.

Tom and Rodge made for the corner of the house again, making sure that they couldn't be seen from the dining room window where it was most likely that Miss Maybury would be sitting and looking out. It was still very light. With Tom leading the way they climbed up the ivy, scrambled over the balustrade on to the balcony and disappeared through the window, carefully closing it behind them.

Sarah settled down to wait for darkness. The sky along the river turned vivid red. It wouldn't be long now.

As the light faded, she listened intently for any sound. The disturbing thought came to her that Edmund Cope might decide to conceal himself in the same shrub to wait for darkness. That would be disconcerting for both of them! She put the thought hastily aside.

It was becoming dark. She saw the gaslight flicker on in the dining room and tensed herself still more. But nothing stirred in the shrubbery.

A silvery moon came up. It was very beautiful but Sarah was becoming too cramped to appreciate it. She was longing to stand up. Looking across to the shrub where Graham was hidden she wondered if he were as stiff as she was and whether he was getting fed up. And she wondered precisely where Tom and Rodge were hiding. She didn't envy them.

She had now given up expecting anything to happen that night. She was only puzzled that Tom and Rodge weren't admitting defeat and emerging from the house again. She didn't feel she could come out of her hiding place until they did. But what was keeping them?

A rustle from Graham's shrub showed that he, too, was restless and moving about. Then the branches parted and he emerged. His dark shape came crawling towards her. 'There's no point –' he began to hiss at her, then stopped.

They had both seen it, a pinpoint of light flickering on and off from the darkness of the balcony window. For a moment Sarah couldn't understand what it was. Then she realised. It was one of the boys, signalling to them with a torch in Morse code. Graham was staring at it.

'What's he saying?' she hissed to Graham.

'C-O-P-E, Cope. D-O-W-N-S-T-A-I-R-S, Downstairs.'

They peered at each other's faces in the darkness as the light stopped flickering and realisation dawned.

'He's inside the house already,' hissed Graham, incredulously.

'He – he's changed his tactics!' said Sarah. 'Then – he must have been there for ages. Oh, why didn't we – ?'

Suddenly, from somewhere inside the house could be heard a tremendous banging.

11

Pursuit by Moonlight

For a moment, Sarah and Graham froze, unsure whether to stay at their posts or find out what was happening in the house. Then, as the banging started again after a brief pause, Sarah jumped to her feet.

'I can't stand not knowing what's going on,' she said and she started to run towards the terrace. Graham came after her. As she raced up the steps, she realised that in addition to the banging she could hear faintly a raised voice, pleading and sobbing; Miss Maybury's voice. Then other voices shouting. She was so keyed up and fearful for the old lady that she had forgotten any fears for herself.

The dining room was empty but the gaslight was on and the french windows unlocked. Sarah and Graham dashed straight through and into the hall. Tom, dishevelled and harassed, was coming out of the corridor which led off it.

'What are you doing here?' he hissed. 'You're supposed to be outside, watching the back –'

'But – Miss Maybury –' began Sarah.

'She's all right – upset but all right. I'll tell you what happened afterwards, but for now get back! I'm going out the front.' He darted towards the front door.

Sarah glimpsed Miss Maybury along the corridor. She was standing outside a closed door, back towards Sarah, stick in hand. She seemed to be shaking. Rodge was gripping the handle of the door and was listening at it.

'What on earth's been happening?' said Sarah, but Graham was already turning to run back the way they had come. For a moment, despite what Tom had said, she was tempted to go to Miss Maybury. Then, impressed by the anxious tone of Tom's voice, she decided she'd better follow instructions. She went after Graham.

She and Graham saw him the instant they stepped out on to the terrace again. He was sauntering down the lawns towards the river in the moonlight, a debonair, athletic figure in boater and blazer. Edmund Cope, back from the past. The shock brought both of them to a sudden, paralysed halt.

And then, reaching the landing-stage, he turned and was looking at them. His own face was in shadow but he must have seen both of them quite clearly. However, he gave no sign of it. Still unhurried, he stepped off the landing-stage and Sarah realised that there must be a boat there. She heard the gentle splash of oars as he rowed away.

Graham unfroze.

'He's had a boat tied up there all the time!' he muttered. 'All the time we've been hiding in the bushes he must have been inside the house ... and now he's got out again!'

He started forward. 'I'm going after him. That's what we're here for, isn't it?'

Sarah really admired Graham just then. If it weren't for his example she was sure her own courage would have failed her. But she wasn't going to be outdone.

'I'm coming, too,' she said, and she ran after him down to the river. They halted on the bank.

He was rowing upstream towards Hamblesey, about to round the bend in the river and disappear from sight. Sarah realised that this was the same view that Miss Maybury must have had the last time she had ever seen Edmund Cope. Except that then it had been golden sunshine. Now he was rowing into black shadow under the archway of willow trees.

But they weren't in shadow. They were in brilliant moonlight. He must be able to see them clearly and yet still he gave no sign. His rowing was unhurried.

'We can't follow on foot, it's like a jungle in that direction,' rapped Graham. 'Help me get the boat out.' He dashed towards the boathouses.

It was the boat they had been out in earlier. Together

they scrambled it into the water and jumped in.

'Shall I take an oar?' asked Sarah.

'No it's better if I have both,' he said.

Graham strained at the oars as they drifted out into the middle, putting every ounce of energy he had into it.

'Don't want to boast, but I *am* this year's junior singles champion at the club,' he said fiercely. 'Should give him a run for his money.'

'But what do we do if we catch him?' thought Sarah weakly.

There was no sign of the other two boys as they passed the boundary wall. There just hadn't been a chance to let them know what was happening.

It was eerie to be gliding along in the near darkness, Graham heaving rhythmically at the oars. He seemed like a machine but the strain showed on his face. Sarah peered into the dimness ahead, watching for any sign that they were catching up with their quarry.

Surely they had to be. He had been rowing so casually, so slowly, while Graham was racing along. But they rounded bend after bend in the river and there was no sign of him.

It became difficult to believe that he was still there ahead of them and occasionally Graham rested on the oars for a moment to listen. Each time, faintly, they heard the soft plop and creak of the oars, always the same distance in front or even perhaps a little further away. And always sounding relaxed, steady and slow. Each time, Graham frantically redoubled his efforts until:

'I – I just can't go on any more,' he gasped, red-faced and haggard, reluctantly admitting defeat. He drew the oars into the boat and leaned forward, chest heaving, struggling for breath.

'Listen!' whispered Sarah, sharply.

They both sat motionless.

'I can't hear him any more,' she said softly.

There was silence except for the slapping of the water around the boat. Dipping the oars gently into the water again, Graham rowed quietly onwards. They were both

84

still listening, Sarah peering ahead into the darkness. Had he outpaced them? Or had he stopped? Was he lying in wait ...

The water in front was suddenly lit by brilliant moonlight as the river emerged from the trees. 'Look,' said Sarah, 'a boat.'

She had almost missed seeing it. It was moored to a little wooden landing-stage that was almost obscured by a willow that seemed to grow out of it.

What the landing-stage was doing there in the middle of nowhere, Sarah couldn't imagine. There was no house, just the woods that lined the river for miles.

'Is it *his* boat?' said Graham, mystified. 'If it is – where's he gone?' He pulled in and grabbed the post of the landing-stage. Like the one at Lockets it was old and rotting.

'Solid enough boat, anyway,' he said. 'My hand doesn't go through it or anything.' He was touching it gingerly as if he thought it might.

'I'll take a look on the bank,' said Sarah, and she scrambled ashore. She wasn't really feeling very bold but she thought she ought to justify her weight in the boat.

She stood nervously on the bank in the moonlight, wondering what she was looking for and trying to repress the fear that he was concealed behind a tree, waiting to spring out on her. She walked slowly forward, carefully lifting aside some brambles to do so.

She was walking on something hard and irregular. Looking down she realised that it was bricks. She was treading on the foundations of what had once been a cottage.

'Here!' exclaimed Graham behind her. 'There are letters carved into this post I'm holding on to. It says "Willow Cottage".'

She was standing on the foundations of the cottage in which Edmund Cope had lived during the summer of 1914. They both looked at the boat they had followed, floating innocently beneath the willow tree.

*

85

Graham seemed to have forgotten his hostility towards her as they rowed back.

'I suppose I didn't really believe it,' he said once, in an awe-struck voice, 'but now I've seen him for myself and – it's like Tom said, if it's not a ghost, who is it? And what's he doing it for?'

Sarah was remembering the languorous way in which the figure had walked down to the river and then got into the boat and rowed away. He hadn't run or even hurried. There'd been something unearthly about it. He hadn't seemed in the same world as them.

'I don't believe in ghosts,' she said, 'and yet at the same time it just *was* Edmund Cope.'

'So he went to the place where Willow Cottage used to be and then disappeared!' said Tom. 'That's fantastic!'

'If that *was* his boat moored to the landing-stage,' said Sarah.

'Whose else would it be, tied up in the middle of no-where?' said Rodge.

Tom and Rodge had been anxiously waiting for them by the boathouse. Tom had realised where they'd disappeared to when he'd gone round to the back of the house, just in time to hear the sound of their oars fading into the distance.

'Anyway,' he said, 'you two have saved the evening from being a complete disaster. Miss Maybury wants to see us. I think she's pretty upset by what's happened.'

'Why? What did happen in the house?' said Sarah, alarmed.

Tom and Rodge explained as they put the boat away. They had hidden themselves away upstairs as planned. While in their hiding places they'd both heard the sounds of someone moving around below them and had supposed it to be Miss Maybury, until they had suddenly heard her voice.

'We heard her calling out,' Tom recalled. 'She was saying "Edmund, Edmund, is that you?" – things like that. It made my hair stand on end. That's when we both realised what idiots we were, waiting for him to come into the house – all the time we were sitting around making our plans he was in there already, and downstairs!'

'We didn't know what to do,' said Rodge. 'The plan was just to see what he was up to and then follow him. But, of course, since he'd got bolder and gone downstairs – and before dark, as well – we started to wonder if Miss Maybury was in danger.'

'At least, I did –'

'So did I,' said Tom. 'We just listened for a time wondering what to do and then suddenly there was this tremendous banging and we could hear Miss Maybury yelling and sobbing – couldn't make out what she was saying, but it sounded terrible – and I couldn't stand it any longer. I just had to find out if she needed some help.'

'But when we got downstairs we found her banging on a door with her stick. She'd been trying to open it to see if Edmund Cope was in there, but it was locked ...'

'And that's when you turned up,' said Rodge. 'Tom went racing round to the front of the house to see if he could see anything through the window – he's got more nerve than I have – but the window was open and the room was empty.'

'He – he'd got out of the window and walked calmly back to his boat,' said Sarah, 'which is when we saw him.'

'He must have been in the house a long time,' said Rodge. 'I wonder what he was doing? I wonder *why* he changed his tactics.'

'And – and I wonder why Miss Maybury lost her head like that?' said Sarah, as they climbed the steps. 'It doesn't sound like her.'

'Perhaps we're going to find out,' said Tom.

Miss Maybury was in the sitting room, seated in one of the armchairs. She didn't turn her head as they entered. The unsteady glow of the gaslight was behind her and her face was in shadow.

'Miss Maybury,' said Sarah, timidly, after a few moments, 'Miss Maybury, I –'

'You disturbed him,' said the old lady suddenly and

87

her voice was shaking. 'You disturbed him and he may never come back.'

'But –'

'When you first came here you promised me that you would not tell the police about my visitor. Now I want you to promise me that you will never again do what you did tonight. That if – if he ever should come back, you won't interfere.'

'I'm sorry if we blundered, Miss Maybury,' said Tom, unhappily, 'but we were scared you might be in some sort of danger –'

'Promise,' said Miss Maybury. She was close to tears but there was iron in her voice.

'How can you be sure you're not – ?' began Sarah.

'Promise!'

They looked at each other. There was no alternative.

'We promise,' they said.

'Batty!' growled Graham beneath his breath. He sounded enraged.

'And now,' said Miss Maybury, 'I'd like to be left alone to think over what happened tonight.'

But Sarah couldn't go just like that. She had to make sure they'd be able to keep some sort of eye on the old lady.

'All right, Miss Maybury,' she said, 'we won't interfere without your permission again. But we can come back and tidy up the house and grounds, can't we? You did say we could.'

Waiting anxiously for a reply, Sarah didn't see the look of utter fury that flashed across Graham's face. Her words had brought him to snapping point.

12

The Big Bust-Up

Miss Maybury's expression softened.

'You may come back,' she said. 'Yes, of course you may. I'd like you to, I'd be grateful.'

Sarah sighed with relief. And then Miss Maybury reached out and took her hand and patted it.

'I hope you don't think I was being ungrateful to make you promise like that. But it means such a lot to me.'

She looked at Sarah anxiously before releasing her hand and leaned back in her chair again.

'Of course, I understand that you were worried about me – I did behave badly, screaming and banging like that. I couldn't help it after I'd heard his voice –'

'His voice!' said Sarah, alertly, 'you mean he *spoke* to you?'

'He called my name. Constance. Three times. He was on the other side of the door.'

Sarah and Tom looked at each other, startled.

'Miss Maybury,' said Tom, 'did you recognise the voice?'

'There was no mistaking it,' said Miss Maybury. 'It was *his*. There was never another one like it.'

It was little wonder there'd been such a disturbance. She believed she'd heard the voice of Edmund Cope. A voice from the dead.

Sarah looked round at the others. Tom and Rodge were staring at Miss Maybury. Graham was glowering.

'It's very late,' said Sarah, 'we'd better go, hadn't we? We'll come back tomorrow.'

'Not tomorrow,' said Miss Maybury. 'I'd like to rest and be quiet tomorrow ... and think.'

'But –'

'You may come back the next day.'

'All right, Miss Maybury,' said Sarah reluctantly. 'The next day.'

'Well!' Rodge exploded as soon as they were outside. 'What did you make of that? Do you think she imagined it?'

'She hasn't imagined anything else, has she?' said Tom tersely. 'We've just proved that for ourselves.'

'But whose voice was it? How would anybody except her even know what Edmund Cope's voice sounded like?'

Sarah, Tom and Rodge walked slowly along the drive together, making for their bikes. They were so preoccupied by what Miss Maybury had told them that they didn't notice that Graham had shot away by himself and was striding along ahead. By the time they reached their bikes, he was astride his.

'We didn't tell her where we followed Edmund Cope to,' said Sarah.

'Best not tell her *anything* till we've found out for ourselves what's happening,' said Tom. 'It'd only excite her more.'

He looked at Rodge.

'What about us two finding this Willow Cottage place on foot first thing tomorrow morning and seeing if the boat's still there?'

'Good idea!' said Rodge.

'Then we can have a meeting at HQ to discuss the whole thing and decide what to do next. Ten o'clock tomorrow morning all right?'

'You're all talking,' said Graham tensely, 'as if we've got any choice about what we do next.'

Everybody looked at him. He had the dangerous air of an unexploded bomb.

'What do you mean?' asked Tom.

'You're all as batty as Miss Maybury. All I know is that just as it gets interesting we've been warned not to interfere – and we've given our promise not to. And not to come at all tomorrow. Instead my services as a housemaid and jobbing gardener are are being offered around. Without my permission being asked, of course.' He glanced at Sarah.

'Tidy up the grounds!' he said scathingly. 'With a ghost at large getting bolder every day!'

He rode off.

'Graham, wait!' yelled Tom. 'What are you talking about? What do *you* think we should do?'

'See you in the morning,' shouted Graham, 'I don't feel like talking about it any more tonight.'

'He's in a bad temper,' muttered Tom, as Graham's light disappeared round a bend. 'I expect he'll be all right in the morning.' He looked at Sarah. 'You mustn't think badly of Graham. He's not usually like this.'

'I know. Only when I'm around,' thought Sarah.

She had a feeling of foreboding. She didn't think Graham would be 'all right' in the morning. He'd had a very determined look about him and she wondered just what he was going to do.

The feeling of foreboding persisted as she cycled home and put her bike away. Then she decided she had to throw it off.

'I'm being silly,' she thought. 'After all, we seemed to get on very well when we were in the boat together.'

She noticed some bits of carpet in the shed.

'I know. I'll go to the HQ early tomorrow morning and smarten the place up. Show them how nice it can be. Give them all a surprise – especially Graham.'

In the dining room at Lockets, Miss Maybury sat in her chair by the window, gazing out unseeing into the darkness. She had quite recovered her poise.

'He will come back,' she told herself. 'I know he will. I think it will be tomorrow.'

Sarah's dreams that night were a strange jumble. She didn't know whether it was 1914 or the present day. She was at Lockets which was dominated by the giant presence of Edmund Cope, but when she managed to see his features she discovered he was really Tom in a boater and blazer. Miss Maybury's father was in the house, too, a stern figure. She was very frightened of him and wondered what he was going to do. Then she realised that he was Graham in disguise. She herself was wearing that lovely dress of Miss Maybury's.

When she woke in the morning she was wondering again why Edmund Cope had not come to that meeting with Miss Maybury in 1914 ...

At ten o'clock, Sarah opened the door of the clubhouse to Tom and Rodge.

'Did you find Willow Cottage and see the boat?' she asked them.

'We found Willow Cottage all right —' said Rodge.

'But we didn't see the boat for the simple reason that it isn't there any longer,' finished Tom. 'Unless you were imagining things last night, it's gone. I don't know. I just don't understand what's happening.'

'Well, Graham and I weren't imagining things,' said Sarah, firmly, 'but before we get down to business, come and look inside the clubhouse and be ready for a surprise. The decorators are in.'

'Well, of all the —' said Tom, as he followed her in. 'I thought I was in the wrong place for a second.' He looked round in astonishment.

The place had been cleaned up. But, more than that, there was a carpet on the floor. Well, not exactly *a* carpet, but several bits of carpet which hadn't yet been tacked together but had been cut to fit against each other so neatly that it didn't really matter that they weren't all of the same pattern or even colour.

The windows were sparkling and screwed to the wooden lintel above them was a curtain rail which until recently had been in the sitting room of Sarah's home. She had rescued it from the dustbin and her father had cut it down for her. Some cheerful red curtains were hanging from it. They, too, had come from the sitting room.

'They're much too big for here,' said Sarah. 'I'm going to cut them down but I just wanted to see what they looked like first. I'll stitch the bits of carpet together as well.'

'They look terrific!' said Tom.

'Fab – u – lous!' said Rodge, who was gazing round in admiration.

'It's only a start,' said Sarah. 'It'll take a bit of time to get the place looking really good. I'd like to paint the walls.'

'My parents are doing some decorating just now,' said Rodge, entering into the spirit of things. 'Maybe they'll have some paint left over.'

Sarah was delighted by the boys' enthusiasm. It hadn't been all that easy begging the curtains and off-cuts of carpets, especially as her mother had been livid about the time she'd arrived home last night. After that she'd had to persuade Dad to dump off all the stuff at the top of the lane, on his way to work in the car, and then Sarah had carried it down to the clubhouse in stages after she'd arrived by bike.

'There's a new picture on the wall,' said Tom. 'Did you put it up?'

'Yes,' said Sarah. 'I – I thought it might appeal to Graham.' She almost had the grace to blush.

'I didn't think you'd want to sit and look at it yourself,' said Tom, grinning, 'but it is pretty good.'

It was a big, unframed picture of a first world war aircraft – a Sopwith Camel it explained on the back – engaged in a dogfight, the be-goggled pilot peering down out of his cockpit as he banked the aircraft. A smoking German plane was plunging to earth in the background. Sarah had spotted it as she passed the newsagent's shop that morning and promptly bought it. It had been very cheap and she was quite clear about her own motives for buying it. It was the especially nice thing for Graham and she hoped it would help her get around him.

By the way he was grinning, it was obvious that Tom was well aware of her motives.

'Is it only for Graham?' asked Rodge, plaintively, 'or can I have a quick glance at it from time to time?'

'I don't think she'd mind,' said Tom. 'It's just that there's more rejoicing in heaven over one sinner that repenteth ... I hope he likes it, Sarah.'

'I've just remembered,' said Rodge, snapping his fingers. 'Mum and Dad are going to buy a couple of new armchairs. Perhaps I could collar the old ones –'

He stopped. It were as if a chill wind had blown into the room. Sarah looked round and saw that Graham was standing in the doorway.

'Well,' he said. 'Perhaps I'd better go back and get my smoking jacket.'

He walked slowly inside, glaring around.

'And my carpet slippers.'

He obviously wasn't feeling any better this morning and Sarah's heart sank.

'Sarah's brought you a present,' said Tom, nodding towards the picture. 'Specially for you. The rest of us have to ask your permission to look at it.'

Graham glanced at it briefly. 'Not authentic,' he said. He swung round angrily.

'Who says I want our HQ turned into a hotel lounge? Since we vote on everything else why didn't we vote on this?'

'Sarah was only trying to be helpful, Graham,' said Tom. Although he was trying to speak soothingly, there was an edge to his voice. 'I like it and so does Rodge.'

'Oh, dear!' thought Sarah despairingly. 'I wish I'd never thought of it now. I'm making things worse.'

Graham glanced at her but his expression didn't soften. 'I thought we were meeting this morning to talk business,' he said.

'All right,' said Tom resignedly. 'Let's sit down.'

Sarah's feeling of foreboding was back with a vengeance.

'The question is,' said Tom, when they were settled, 'what we do next about Miss Maybury?'

'I haven't changed my mind since last night,' said Graham. 'It's obvious there's only one thing we can do and

if anybody thinks differently they're as batty as she is,'
  'And that is?'
  'Hand the whole thing over to a grown-up who can get something done about it. There's something very peculiar going on at Lockets and I think it's fascinating but I'm not kidding myself any longer there's anything we can do about it. Anyway, we've promised we won't interfere.'
  'No, no, no!' thought Sarah despairingly. This was what, at the back of her mind, she'd been dreading.
  'Anybody else think that?' Tom was saying.
  'We *can't*,' said Sarah. 'We *promised* her we wouldn't tell anybody.'
  'You promised you wouldn't tell the police. That's not who I'm thinking of.'
  'Who *are* you thinking of telling?' asked Tom.
  'The Skipper.'
  'The Skipper.' Tom rose to his feet.
  'That's right.' Hero worship shone out of Graham's eyes. 'He'll be at the rowing club this morning. He'd know how to handle this. He knows how to handle everything.'
  Sarah jumped to her feet.
  'That wouldn't be playing fair by Miss Maybury,' she protested desperately. 'She meant us not to tell *anybody*, whatever the actual promise.'
  'Oh, for goodness' sake! What's it matter anyway what daft promises you've made. Don't you realise Miss Maybury might be in *danger*? I expect he *will* tell the police, in fact, but that'll be for him to decide.'
  'Graham could be right, you know,' said Tom, uneasily. 'Miss Maybury does live in a world of her own. Perhaps we oughtn't to pay too much attention to what she says!'
  Sarah could see that Rodge was impressed, too. And maybe, logically, Graham was right. And yet she *knew* ...
  'Please, Graham,' she said, 'I don't think you realise how precious all this is to Miss Maybury. All right – it's cranky to have sat there all these years waiting for her dead sweetheart to come back to her. But it's all she's got and she'd rather have anything than people from the modern world tramping into the house and ruining her dream.

She'd rather be dead, I know she would. Graham, you *mustn't* tell anybody.'

Sarah hadn't realised it but she was raising her voice, almost shouting.

'Mustn't?' Graham shouted back, furiously. 'You've only been in the Club ten minutes. You're not even a proper member but you're already yelling at me and telling us what to do.'

'Calm down, Graham,' said Tom. 'Let's put it to the vote.'

'I'm not voting because I'm not in the Club any more,' shouted Graham. 'I'm going to tell the Skipper now because I'm certain it's the right thing to do.'

'Graham,' said Sarah, as he walked towards the door. 'I'm not yelling now. Please don't.'

He halted in the doorway and looked back.

'You only joined us for this business at Lockets, didn't you,' he said bitterly, 'so you won't be staying much longer. I'll come back to the Club when you've gone. Not before.'

She watched him ride away. She felt like the pilot of the burning German plane in the picture.

13

The Ghost Walks at Noon

So that was that: the end of the Clover Club as far as Sarah was concerned. She'd known, of course, that her membership was only a temporary affair, but nevertheless the shock of it was so great that all other thoughts were driven out of her mind for the moment.

Tom and Rodge were trying to make comforting noises.

'Graham'll come round,' Tom was saying. 'Give him time.'

'We'll patch things up,' said Rodge.

'It's no use,' said Sarah, 'I may as well go now.'

'*Now*? Don't be crazy, Sarah! There's no need for that –'

'We're all going to Lockets tomorrow, aren't we? We can go without Graham –'

'Now who's being crazy?' said Sarah. 'You three are a trio. All I seem to do is get in the way and cause rows.'

'But Sarah –' She was touched to hear how really upset Tom sounded. But she could tell that even he knew it wouldn't be any good.

'It would only spoil things if I were to keep on hanging around, with Graham not wanting me,' she said. 'The Club wouldn't be the same. I really think I ought to go now.'

They could tell she meant it. And they knew she was right.

'What about the carpets and curtains and pictures,' said Rodge, gloomily.

'Keep them as a parting gift.'

Almost certainly Graham would throw them out the next time he came, but she didn't care. They just seemed silly now. Or worse than silly. They'd probably been the last straw as far as Graham was concerned. He probably wanted his toffee papers and filthy windows back.

'It may be that Graham *is* right about telling the Skipper, though,' Tom said as they walked out of the door with her.

'No, he's not,' she said with certainty. But she didn't want to argue any more. There was nothing she could do to stop it, so what was the point?

'The Skipper's pretty dynamic,' said Rodge. 'I expect he'll have the police in straight away.'

'Skipper, Skipper, Skipper!' She was fed up with hearing the name. She wished she'd never heard of him. 'Oh, Miss Maybury, we've betrayed you,' she thought as she got on her bike. But then she thrust the whole thing out of her mind. It was too awful even to think about.

She found herself astride her bike looking at Tom and Rodge and not knowing what to say.

'This is stupid,' said Tom desperately. 'Let's at least have a farewell treat together. I'll buy you both whatever you fancy in Garnetts.'

Sarah hesitated. Was it any use prolonging it?

Garnetts was a sort of glutton's delight. They sold the best pastries in Cherringham, smothered in the richest real cream. And so as to save you the agony of waiting till you got home before eating them, there was a restaurant and coffee bar on the premises. Or if it were sunny, like today, they'd put tables out on the terrace overlooking the river. It was a gem of a place. Sarah managed to persuade her mother into taking her there about once a year as a special treat.

'All right,' she said, 'how could any girl resist an invitation like that?'

'You two wait here,' said Tom. 'I'll lock up and be with you in a tick.'

It should have been a glorious outing on a day like this. They cycled into Cherringham, leaned their bikes against the guard-rail running along the river bank and sat down at one of the tables on the terrace. Sarah had a concoction which involved some melting pastry, much cream and raspberries. Together with Garnetts' special coffee it ought to have been delicious. But somehow it didn't taste all that good.

She couldn't get it out of her mind that when she'd finished and the waitress came to take the plates away, she'd have to start saying good-bye all over again. It was probably foolish of her to have come. The boys were very quiet, too.

And there was Miss Maybury ...

There was a wire litter-basket on a lamp-post nearby and Rodge idly got up and went over to it, taking out an empty glass bottle to examine it. Then he put it back.

'Just seeing if it was anything of interest,' he said, sitting down again, 'but it's not. Just an ordinary medicine bottle.'

'Sarah doesn't know about our interest in old bottles,' said Tom, 'so that must have been double Dutch to her.' He glanced at Rodge inquiringly. 'Should we tell her?'

'Why not?' said Rodge. 'We've all been keeping the Skipper's secret so faithfully, while there's Graham rushing off to tell him Miss Maybury's. Not fair, really, is it? Should be tit-for-tat.'

'That's what I think,' said Tom.

'Bottles? Skipper?' inquired Sarah, surfacing from her thoughts about Miss Maybury.

'We're talking about the secret job we're doing for the Skipper in the woods near Lockets,' said Tom. 'You know – what we were working at when we first saw you. Will you keep it secret if we tell you?'

'I don't give away other people's secrets,' said Sarah levelly and regretted it as she saw Tom wince. It wasn't his fault.

'We're looking for a bottle dump. Still are.'

'Bottle dump?'

'An old rubbish dump that's been in use for centuries. We'd hope to find a lot of antique bottles and pot lids there. Be worth a lot of money if we could find it and sell all the stuff to collectors. The Skipper wants the money to buy a new boat for the rowing club.'

'But why all the secrecy?'

'The Skipper says there are some proper bottle collectors nosing around,' said Rodge. 'If they just get wind we're on to a new site, they'll work all night to find it and strip it.'

'We haven't had any luck yet,' said Tom.

'What makes the Skipper think there's a dump in those woods?' asked Sarah, idly.

'He's been ransacking old records to find out where the local dump used to be and he's come up with some clues. It sounds an interesting thing to do – like being a detective. What we're looking for is a carving on a stone, of all things.'

'Carving on a stone! What sort of carving?'

'Dunno. That's the only reference the Skipper's been able to find. Comes from some old book, apparently.'

'What's the metal detector for?'

'That was our idea. If there's a buried rubbish dump there ought to be some metal amongst it.'

'Looking for a stone with a carving on, in those woods,' said Rodge with a sigh, 'is like looking for a needle in a haystack. The place is strewn with slabs of stone, once you start looking. But hardly the sort of stones you'd expect to find carvings on.'

'It may be that the stone with the carving on was taken away donkey's years ago,' said Tom, gloomily. 'I think the metal detector's a better bet.'

A carving on a stone. Sarah had the feeling that she'd come across that phrase before. But she was preoccupied again. She was gazing along the river bank, a pedestrian precinct at this point, to where the traffic in Cherringham's High Street turned away from the river.

A police panda car had come to halt at the zebra crossing and she could see the two policemen inside, shirt-sleeved because of the hot weather, gazing idly ahead. She was thinking that perhaps they would be the very police-men who would go to investigate the strange events at Lockets and interview the funny old lady who lived there.

She started to picture the scene in her mind. The car cruising up the drive, putting to an end the brooding stillness which had hung over Lockets for so long, the ratchet-noise of the handbrake and slam of doors, the policemen looking about them saying 'What sort of place is this?' Banging at the door, questioning Miss Maybury, taking solemn notes, patiently and kindly explaining that what she is suggesting is quite impossible and has she ever thought she might get an old person's flat in town? Miss Maybury, frightened, pathetic, bewildered, her little dream-world shattered and made foolish.

'What am I doing sitting here brooding over my own troubles!' thought Sarah, suddenly rigid, despising herself for having done nothing so far.

She jumped to her feet, her coffee only half-finished.

'Thanks ... Tom ... Rodge ... that really was nice. But I have to go to Lockets now and explain to Miss Maybury what might happen. I have to give her some warning. I have to tell her that I've let her down –'

She made for her bike before the boys could say anything, just in case they tried to talk her out of it. But as she got on, she found that Tom was by her side.

'We're coming with you, whether you like it or not,' he said. 'Miss Maybury isn't only your business you know. She's ours as well.'

'And we've got as much explaining to do as you have,' said Rodge. 'After all, we've both got to like her.'

There was nothing she could say.

It was about half past eleven as they rode out of Cherringham.

At about a quarter to twelve on that hot summer morning, Miss Maybury was seated, as always, by the french windows in the dining room gazing out towards the river when a tremor suddenly ran through her like an electric shock.

An oarsman was coming into view from the Hamblesey direction, a young man in a boater and striped blazer, rowing vigorously. As she peered at him, he pulled in towards the landing-stage. He was out of sight behind it for a few moments as he tied up. Then he reappeared suddenly, leaping athletically out of the boat. He waved.

Miss Maybury struggled to her feet, gasping and putting her weight on to her stick, fumbling to open the french window so that she would be able to see more clearly.

He was walking up the lawns towards her. As he saw her at the window he took off his boater and waved it gaily, revealing the mass of shining golden hair that seemed to blaze in the sunshine like a halo.

He stopped below the terrace, looking up at her as she stood there as if paralysed. Miss Maybury heard again that rich, deep voice.

'Constance. I've come back.'

Two world wars had come and gone while Miss Maybury had waited. England beyond Lockets had changed beyond recognition while she dreamed.

But her moment had come at last.

At the front door a few minutes later, Sarah banged the knocker for the third time but there was no reply.

'She's probably sitting by the window at the back of the house,' said Tom. 'Let's go round there.'

'At least the police don't seem to be here yet,' said Sarah. 'I was scared they might be.'

As they made their way round the side of the house they came in sight of the river and Sarah had an impression of widening ripples on the water. The significance of it, that an oarsman had passed out of sight behind the trees only moments ago, didn't occur to her.

There was no sign of Miss Maybury when they reached the terrace. She wasn't sitting in her usual place. Sarah led the way up the steps and opened the french doors.

'Miss Maybury!' she cried in alarm.

The old lady was seated at the table, her head bent over it and cradled in her arms. For a moment, Sarah thought she was ill or unconscious. Thoroughly alarmed, she hurried towards her, followed by the boys.

Then she realised that Miss Maybury was quietly weeping.

Had the police been after all? Or the Skipper?

'Miss Maybury. What's happened? Are you all right?'

The old lady raised her head and Sarah saw that from where she was sitting she was able to see herself in the long mirror over the sideboard.

'Edmund has been here,' she said. 'Just a few moments ago. He spoke to me.'

For a moment Sarah felt as if she were reeling giddily.

'Edmund? Edmund Cope?'

'Yes.'

He had come here, almost at noon, in the dazzling sunlight?

'What did he say, Miss Maybury?' asked Tom.

'He wants to meet me, in our secret place in the woods, at one o'clock.'

'Meet you? Face to face?'

'Yes.'

One o'clock was just over an hour away. For Sarah, the world reeled again.

'And his voice, Miss Maybury,' said Tom, 'what did it sound –?'

'It was *his* voice.'

Sarah had forgotten everything else now. The quarrel with Graham ... the police ... the Skipper ... even that she was no longer a member of the Clover Club. All became insignificant beside the stunning fact that what Miss Maybury had waited for for so long seemed to have come true.

But if it had come true, why –?

Sarah knelt down beside the old lady and took her hand. 'Miss Maybury,' she said, 'then why are you crying?'

But Miss Maybury was gazing at her reflection and Sarah suddenly knew the answer before she spoke.

'It does matter what I see in the mirror, after all,' she said.

Sarah could read her mind. She had lived with her dream for most of her life. But she wasn't really batty. In her heart she knew that she couldn't really make time stand still as she'd wanted it to. Her mirror showed her that.

Poor Miss Maybury! Her dream was so fragile. It could be destroyed so easily, even by the very fact of its appearing to come true.

'I'm so very glad you've come back to me today, after all,' said the old lady. 'Despite the fact that I was so rude to you last night, I wonder – I wonder if I could ask you to do something else for me?'

'Anything, Miss Maybury,' said Sarah fervently, 'anything.'

But she wasn't prepared for what was to come.

'If I give you directions and tell you how to get to our secret dell, would *you* meet Edmund in my place?'

14

Sarah Goes to the Dell

'Go in your place!' said Sarah, dumbfounded, 'but –'

'I'm an old woman,' said Miss Maybury, wistfully. 'It's many years since I left this house and I don't think I could even reach the dell where Edmund and I used to meet.'

She was gazing at her reflection in the mirror again.

'And even if I could . . . look at me . . .'

Her voice had dropped to a whisper.

'But you, in the dress and hat you wore the other day . . . it would be as if I were young again . . . it would be just like it was . . . and you could come back and tell me . . .'

And Sarah knew that behind it all, Miss Maybury was afraid to go herself in case her dream were finally destroyed, as she feared it would be. She wanted Sarah to find out what was happening first.

Tom was making signals, stepping out on the terrace with Rodge. She joined them.

'Battier than ever,' whispered Rodge.

'No,' said Tom, 'not really. Deep down she's as mystified as we are and she doesn't want the pretending to come to an end. But she's terrified it's going to.'

'Yes,' said Sarah.

'What do you think of going in her place?' asked Tom, watching her closely. He seemed to be able to see the answer in her face.

'I – I suppose I ought to,' she said. 'She wants me to go so badly. And anyway it's probably the only way we'll find out what's going on. The only trouble is, having said all that –'

She suddenly buried her face in Tom's shoulder.

'I think my knees are actually knocking. I'm terrified.

You see, after all this, I think I've decided that I do believe in ghosts, after all.'

'If it's the ghost of Edmund Cope,' said Tom, 'I don't suppose you could wish for a nicer one. You'd have every ghostly Edwardian lady envying you.'

'I'm serious, Tom.'

'I know. But if Rodge and I are lying hidden watching this meeting place, will you dare to go then?'

'We wouldn't let anybody hurt you, Sarah,' said Rodge.

She looked at them. And they looked back at her.

'Do you trust us?' said Tom.

'Yes,' said Sarah. 'All right.'

At twenty minutes to one a slim young figure in the fashions of 1914 stepped out on to the terrace of Lockets and, picking up her skirt with one hand, descended the steps on to the lawn. Sarah was on her way to a rendezvous with a ghost.

She walked down to the wrought-iron gate at the end of the garden through which she had peered on her first visit to the house. Half an hour earlier the boys had freed the rusted bolts for her and now she was able to open it easily and step out into the woodland by the willow tree in which she'd sat. It must have been the first time the gate had been opened for many years . . .

The boys had gone on ahead, straight after freeing the gate. Miss Maybury had given them careful instructions where to find the meeting place and by now they should be hidden and keeping it under observation. If 'Edmund Cope' were to arrive very early they would be ready and waiting.

Miss Maybury herself had watched Sarah until she disappeared through the gate. Now she sat down again to wait.

'Let it be Edmund,' she said fiercely to herself, once, but otherwise she remained motionless.

Sarah picked her way to the woods where she had first seen the boys. It was quite difficult finding her way because, although Miss Maybury had given her detailed instructions, the woods were now so overgrown that the footpaths were hard to find, and she continually had to make detours. In particular she had to avoid tearing her skirt on the brambles.

Although she was extremely frightened at the prospect that lay in front of her, she was also becoming oddly elated. As she proceeded she found it more and more difficult not to believe that this was the golden summer of 1914. She surrendered herself to the feeling that she was Constance Maybury, daughter of a wealthy family living in a beautiful country house, on her way to a secret meeting with the glamorous Greek-god-like poet, Edmund Cope.

She had passed the place where the boys had been searching for their bottle dump. Ahead of her was the avenue of ash trees. Miss Maybury had told her to watch out for them. She proceeded down the avenue and at the end of it turned left between bushes, gradually bearing to the right.

Suddenly she was in a dell, a mossy hollow into which the sun slanted through the silver birch trees that surrounded it. It was Miss Maybury's secret dell, rendezvous of many meetings.

A moss-covered slab of stone jutted out from a little knoll, forming a natural seat and Sarah sat down on it. Her nerves were tingling.

When he came into the dell it might be by any one of several possible ways. Her gaze travelled round. But it was still only six minutes to one.

Tom and Rodge must be somewhere very near, but she had deliberately not looked for them because – who knows? – maybe she herself was being watched and she didn't want to give away their presence.

How short and springy and vividly green the turf was at her feet! Almost like green fur. How sweet the summer scents! To give her hands something to do and to take her mind off the waiting, Sarah began to spread her very long skirt along the slab of stone she was sitting on, obsessively smoothing out every wrinkle. She felt like a picture on a chocolate box.

Three minutes to one.

Panic! What was she doing here? What would he say when he came, expecting to find Miss Maybury waiting for him and finding her instead? What did one say to ghosts anyway? What did they say to you?

Almost without knowing it she began picking at the moss which covered the slab of stone. As she did so she realised she had uncovered the letter 'V' carved on the stone. Curious, despite her fear, she pulled the moss off in swathes. Someone, long ago, had chipped out the words 'I love you'.

Edmund Cope?

It was one o'clock.

A twig crackled somewhere and Sarah froze. She had the feeling that she had never heard so acutely, that she could hear the very spiders and insects moving about among the leaves. But there was no more movement, no other sound. She let her breath out slowly.

It was two minutes past one and he had not yet come.

It was five minutes past one and still he had not come.

At a quarter past one Sarah knew that he wasn't going to come...

At twenty-five past she rose slowly to her feet and left the clearing to start walking back to Lockets. To her surprise, her legs wobbled as if they were made of rubber and it was hard to walk on them. From their places of concealment, Tom and Rodge rose silently to join her. They had seen and heard nothing.

Sarah felt that she had been through a terrible ordeal which she would never want to repeat but it wasn't that which concerned her.

'Why?' she said in utter bewilderment as she re-entered the grounds of Lockets, 'why did he arrange a meeting and then not come? It's cruel.'

Miss Maybury was rising from her chair in the dining room as Sarah entered, her face a mask of eager, trembling, tormented hope. For all her words, she had never really given up hope. Perhaps it really was possible to make time stand still.

'He –' began Sarah, but seeing the expression on Miss Maybury's face she couldn't go on.

The look of hope started to die.

'Did you see him?' asked Miss Maybury.

'He didn't come,' said Sarah, and she put her arm round the old lady in case she should fall.

'Is it a hoax then?' said Sarah. 'Or what is it?'

'A mad, crazy sort of hoax it would be,' replied Tom. 'Whoever could think of a thing like that?'

'Then what is it?' said Sarah despairingly, 'what's going on?'

Sarah, Tom and Rodge were seated on the grass in the front garden by the Victorian swing. Sarah had done her best to comfort Miss Maybury and the old lady seemed to have calmed down. She had told them she wanted to be alone and they had left her in one of the armchairs in the sitting room.

At least the police hadn't turned up yet. Or the Skipper. Or anybody else. Perhaps Graham hadn't carried out his threat after all. Lockets remained in another age. Sarah herself still hadn't changed out of Miss Maybury's dress and hat.

She picked up the book of Edmund Cope's poems which was lying on the grass beside her. She'd got it out of her saddlebag in the vague hope that she might find some clue in it. But it was a very vague hope.

'It's way past lunch time,' said Rodge, gloomily, 'I ought to feel hungry – but I don't.'

On the other side of the house, Miss Maybury opened the french windows and stepped out on to the terrace. She was wearing a hat, the first time she had done so for many years. It was also the first time for many years that she had been outside the house. She had never wanted to go outside, even into the garden. Until now the thought of doing so had even begun to frighten her. But now –

Leaning on her stick, she slowly descended the terrace steps and walked down the lawns to the wrought iron gate, where she paused for a few moments to gather her strength before opening it.

Outside the gate, she paused again, daunted by the sight of the thorns and brambles that lay in her path. It was so different from when she'd last come this way all those years ago. It had been a magic path then, the path that led to Edmund. She hoped it still was.

'I have to go there myself,' she thought. 'It was cowardly of me to ask Sarah. I didn't have faith and of course Edmund wouldn't come if it wasn't me who was there. I should have known that. I must have faith.'

'What's the matter, Sarah?' said Tom, sharply. He had been watching Sarah and had observed her sudden change of expression.

'I think I've got it!' she cried.

'Got what?' said Rodge.

'The answer. The reason for this whole thing.' Sarah was scrambling to her feet, flicking back through the book. 'Tom said the answer might be in the poems and I think it is.'

Tom and Rodge were up on their feet in an instant.

'But – but – I can hardly believe it!' she said. 'It's too incredible.'

'Let's see,' said Rodge.

Sarah was about to turn and show them the book when suddenly she stopped. Her face clouded over and she closed the book instead.

'No. I think we should see Miss Maybury first,' she said. 'There are some things I want to ask her – and it's urgent.'

'But Sarah –'

'Sarah, don't keep us in suspense,' yelled Tom as she set off to run towards the house, holding her skirt clear of the ground with one hand, book in the other.

'Come on,' she shouted, 'it's urgent.' They didn't have any choice but to run in pursuit.

'Sarah, you're driving us crazy!'

But she didn't have any choice about that either. It *was* crazy. She'd found the answer – or thought she had – but she couldn't tell them. Not yet, anyway.

'Miss Maybury,' she called, as she entered the house through the french windows, 'Miss Maybury!'

But the old lady wasn't there.

Miss Maybury was walking doggedly on through the

woods, ignoring the brambles that dragged and tore at her skirt. She had given up trying to go round them. She was too exhausted and dazed. She didn't feel she could keep going much longer but she had to reach that dell. She had to wait there herself, hoping he'd come. All these years of waiting and hoping couldn't have been for nothing. Hope was still all she had to live for. She could never give that up, whatever happened.

But her strength wasn't really up to this. She was gasping hoarsely and she was having difficulty in putting one foot in front of another. The brambles seemed to be like live things dragging her back.

They were clinging now and she couldn't free herself. She tried to pull them away but they tore at her fingers and as she turned and twisted others caught at her. She was nearly at the beginning of the avenue of ash trees.

Sarah and Tom and Rodge found her when they came running through the woods a few minutes later. Sarah had guessed where she might have gone. She had fallen over and was lying still and Sarah had a terrible fear when she first saw her. But it was nothing more than exhaustion.

Tom and Rodge got her out of the brambles, careless of the way they ripped themselves and their clothes on them. Then they helped her to sit up with her back against a tree. Sarah was amazed at how gentle the rather clumsy looking Rodge was with her, sitting with his arm around her shoulders.

She looked so delicate and frail and helpless but, thought Sarah, still beautiful even now. Sarah was blazing with anger.

'I think I know who's responsible for this,' she was thinking, 'and why he's done it. He's cruel, cruel, cruel.'

Out loud she said: 'I'm just going back to the dell to check some things.' Tom and Rodge were attending to the old lady. She deliberately kept her voice level and casual so as not to betray her rage. It would be easy to say too much at the moment before she'd any real evidence.

Before they could reply she was running off along the avenue of ash trees, weaving her way round the brambles and thorns, holding her skirt high. She was going to see if she could get that evidence.

She turned left, once more weaving to the right between bushes, and was in the dell. She halted.

A young man was in there, kneeling, his back towards her. A boater casually on the back of his head, a mass of shining golden hair, a striped blazer, flannels. He was reaching under the slab of stone to take out a metal box which had been concealed there. He was so absorbed that he hadn't heard her.

Her heart was beating very fast, but she was too keyed up and angry for fear.

'Edmund,' she said softly, 'you're late.'

15

Good Old Clover Club

He was on his feet instantly, looking round, taking in the long dress and the hat. They stared at each other in mutual amazement. He was wearing make-up and even at such close quarters she could only just make out who it was under the disguise.

Him! She hadn't expected it to be HIM! Then she'd been wrong after all!

'You're cruel!' she almost sobbed at him. 'Taking advantage of an eccentric old lady! Taking away the only thing she's ever wanted! You haven't cared what happened to her.'

The eeriness of the scene, of the apparent re-creation of the young Miss Maybury and Edmund Cope, seemed to have affected him much more than her and his grip on the box loosened.

She snatched the box and ran, hoping he wouldn't follow. But he did.

'Tom, Rodge!' she screamed as she raced out into the avenue, holding up her dress with one hand. She saw them start to run towards her but her pursuer was coming fast after her now that he'd recovered his wits.

He wanted that box badly. She knew now that everything he had done ... searching the house, setting out to trick Miss Maybury into believing that Edmund Cope had come back to her, arranging the meeting and then not turning up ... all of it had had the object of finding that secret dell, that stone, the box hidden underneath it. And she was pretty certain she knew why.

He mustn't get it back again.

'Tom, Rodge!'

He almost had her. She had to dodge and suddenly she

found that he was between her and the boys. In the confusion, they were on to him.

But he was tough, athletic and more desperate than she could have imagined. Rodge went down to an agonising kick on the shins. Tom hung grimly on but was finally battered away by blows to the head.

Sarah found herself staggering back alone and exhausted, the way she had come, with her pursuer close behind her. She hadn't expected such utter ferocity. He must want that box very, very badly. And it looked as if he were going to get it.

She wouldn't have stood much chance of escape in jeans. In her long skirt it was hopeless. He was right behind her now . . .

'Oh, Miss Maybury,' she thought despairingly, 'I *have* tried.'

Someone loomed in front of her. For a moment it seemed like a mirage. She couldn't believe her eyes. It was Graham.

'Don't worry,' he said, as she staggered level with him, 'I'll stop him.' His gaze was fixed on her pursuer as if he hated him more than anything else in the world. The moment Sarah had passed, he stepped directly into his path.

It was extremely brave of Graham. He was taking on someone much bigger. They crashed to the ground together and went rolling over. As soon as Sarah recovered from her astonishment and exhaustion she turned round to help but there was such a confusion of thrashing limbs that she didn't know what to hit. Graham seemed to be taking a beating but he was hanging on and taking it. Then Tom and Rodge came running up and were piling on.

From the heap came a strangled voice: Graham's.

'Don't be stupid, Skipper,' he said. 'We've all seen you now. We know who you are. So what can you gain from this?'

There was stillness. The man on the ground had stopped struggling. His boater and wig were half off.

'You're right, of course, Graham,' he said, wearily. 'I lost control. But even if I got away with the box I suppose

114

you'd go and report me to the police, wouldn't you?'

'You're dead right,' panted Graham. 'You're so right. If nobody else did, I would.'

'You!' said Tom. 'I don't get it. Of all people – YOU!' Sarah was staring, bewildered.

'But that's not the Skipper,' she said. 'His name's Peter Warden. He's secretary of the Edmund Cope society.'

'Then he's a man of many parts,' said Graham, bitterly, as he got painfully to his feet. 'We only know him through the rowing club and there he's known as the Skipper. Though if you told me he's also Genghis Khan I wouldn't be all that surprised now.'

So she *had* been right. It was the Skipper whom she'd first suspected. That was why she'd been unable to say anything to the boys. It would have been too awful if she'd been wrong . . .

But it hadn't dawned upon her that the Skipper and Peter Warden were one and the same person.

Tom and Rodge were getting up, too. They couldn't take their eyes off Peter Warden. All the ferocity had died out of him. He was sitting with his head in his hands.

'Yes,' said Sarah. That deep, burning rage was still inside her. 'It was him who tried to cheat Miss Maybury out of everything she'd lived for.'

Her words seemed to rouse Peter Warden to anger again. He looked as if he were going to snatch the box and Sarah tightened her grip on it.

'My life's been devoted to Edmund Cope just as much as hers has,' he said. 'It always will be. I wanted what's in there for myself; badly; very badly.'

He heaved himself to his feet, still looking at the box.

'You know what's in there, don't you?' he said to Sarah. 'You must do. You've worked out the clues in Edmund Cope's poems, too.'

'I think I can guess,' said Sarah.

He pulled his wig and boater straight and walked off through the trees in the direction of the river. No-one tried to stop him.

'Well, I never,' said Rodge. 'I'm speechless.'

'I'm not,' said Graham, suspiciously. He was talking with some difficulty because of a swelling lip. 'This job we were doing for the Skipper. Was he really hoping we'd find a bottle dump?'

Sarah didn't really want to add to Graham's humiliation, especially since she was feeling full of admiration for the way he'd tackled Peter Warden. But since he seemed to have guessed, anyway ...

'I don't think so,' she said. 'There's a carved stone in the secret dell. I think that's what he was really hoping you'd find. All the rest was a bluff.'

'Idiots,' yelled Graham. His words carried through the woods. It was as if they were physically striking the disappearing figure of Peter Warden. 'You've made idiots out of us, all along. And I thought you were the greatest.'

Sarah realised that she still didn't know how Graham had come to be there.

'Come on,' said Tom. 'We can think about him later. There's a lot more I'd like to know but I expect we'll find out. We ought to get back to Miss Maybury. She'll be wondering what's going on.'

As they set off back along the avenue of ash trees, he said to Sarah: 'You haven't told us yet what it was you saw in the poems.'

'It was just a line in one of them,' she said. 'The line "a carving on a stone". It was the same phrase you'd used when you told me what the Skipper had asked you to look for. It set my mind working, wondering whether it was a coincidence and I started looking back through the other poems and everything fell into place –'

She glanced at Tom.

'Now if only you'd finished off the book of poems we might have got on to it sooner.'

'Teach me to be more interested in poetry,' he said, and grinned.

'Sarah,' said Rodge, 'what do *you* think is in the box?'

Sarah paused. 'I think we ought to let Miss Maybury tell us that – if she wants to,' she said.

Tom nodded, stopping beside her. 'It's her secret. In fact

I think she really ought to find it where it was hidden.'

'Under the slab of stone in the secret dell,' said Sarah.

Rodge held out his hand.

'Graham and I'll take it there while you bring Miss Maybury along,' he said.

'Guard it well,' said Tom, as he handed it over.

'Why, it's just an old toffee tin with the picture of the King on it,' said Rodge, wonderingly.

Sarah and Tom helped Miss Maybury towards the dell a few minutes later. She was calm, composed, and fully conscious. She had heard nothing of the commotion. Sarah had told her only that they had a surprise for her. She had said nothing about Peter Warden.

She was silent as they neared the dell, drinking in every sight and sound, re-living the journey she had made so often in 1914. Seeing how she peered about her, it brought home to Sarah how short-sighted she was. Peter Warden had played on that when convincing her he was Edmund Cope.

Graham and Rodge stood discreetly to one side. In the entrance to the dell, Miss Maybury halted as if startled and Sarah saw that she was peering at the slab of stone. Sarah realised that from this viewpoint the words 'I love you', carved so large in the stone, stood out very clearly now that the moss had been removed. But surely that should be no surprise to Miss Maybury!

'That wasn't there,' said the old lady. 'It wasn't there when I last met Edmund here.'

'Not there –' began Sarah. Then it dawned on her.

'I can guess when it was carved,' she said. 'It was at the same time that this was put here. He wanted you to see it when you came to the dell. But you never did come.'

Sarah was standing by the slab of stone and, putting her hand deep into the recess beneath, took out the box once more.

'This is the surprise, Miss Maybury,' she said. 'It's been lying here in this very spot ever since the first world war. You were supposed to find it yourself but ... but again, you never did.'

She put it into Miss Maybury's hands as, helped by Tom,

the old lady sat down on the stone.

'I think you'll find it gives you the answer to why Edmund Cope never came back to meet you.'

Graham and Rodge had come silently into the dell and were watching.

Miss Maybury tried to slip back the lid of the box but her hands were trembling. 'Please,' she appealed to Tom.

When he opened it, Sarah saw that inside were some sheets of paper, clipped together and yellowing with age. Miss Maybury took them out.

'It's a letter to me,' she said. 'A letter from Edmund and some poems.' She read through them all, a calm expression on her face, then handed them over to Sarah.

'You may see them if you wish,' she said. 'All of you. But for you I wouldn't have found them.' The boys clustered round.

The top sheet was a letter, closely written on both sides and addressed to 'my own sweetest Constance'. On the other sheets were poems, all dedicated and addressed to Miss Maybury. They were the unpublished work of Edmund Cope and Sarah realised that in terms of money they were probably worth a great deal. Not that money mattered to anybody, certainly not to Peter Warden. She knew that.

When they had finished reading them, Sarah handed them back to Miss Maybury.

'Then it does explain why he never came,' she said sadly.

'Yes,' said Miss Maybury. She was still gazing ahead with that calm expression on her face.

It was a tragic story.

The letter told how Edmund Cope had returned to his cottage from London on that day in 1914. He had been eagerly looking forward to meeting her the next day and then going to ask her father's permission to marry her.

But to his surprise, her father had been waiting for him at the cottage. He told him that his daughter had sent him with a message. She never wanted to see him again. He would listen to nothing, only repeat the message.

Heart-broken, Edmund Cope had left the cottage and returned to London at once. It hadn't occurred to him that her father would be so unscrupulous as to lie.

He had realised the truth only after joining the army and being sent to France. He had met a soldier who came from Cherringham and knew one of the maids at Lockets. The maid had told him that Constance Maybury had become a recluse, broken-hearted over Edmund Cope.

Frantically he had sent letters but they had been returned unopened.

Trying to call on her when on leave he had been turned away by her father and told the police would be informed if he came again.

There had seemed only one way of communicating with her – through his published poems. In desperation, in case he shouldn't survive the war, he decided to try it.

In some of his poems, written at the front line, where he had become a pilot, he poured out all that she meant to him. These poems were for her eyes alone and he put them in the box with a letter, the box that Miss Maybury was now holding.

On his last leave, he had hidden the box in their secret dell, intending that some day she should find it there. On that same visit to the dell, he had carved the words 'I love you' on the stone.

To guide her to the box, he had put hints and clues in his published poems which he hoped she would understand, especially the references to 'our secret place'.

But Miss Maybury never read those published poems. Her parents had even concealed from her the fact that he had published any more after joining the army.

It was only many years later that Peter Warden, and then Sarah, had come to understand the message that lay in the poems.

'My father meant well,' said Miss Maybury now. 'He thought Edmund Cope would break my heart. In his own way he tried to protect me. He didn't realise that he would break both our hearts himself.'

Suddenly Sarah noticed that one tear was rolling down Miss Maybury's cheek. It was a tear of fierce joy and pride. She clutched the papers close to her.

'I knew he would come back to me,' she said, 'and he has. In this letter, in these poems, he's come back.'

The tears were streaming down her face now.

'I knew I was right. I knew he always loved me. He died loving me.'

'So what does Miss Maybury think about the ghost now?' said Rodge. 'You haven't told her it was really the Skipper?'

'I've tried to persuade her it was her imagination,' said Sarah, 'a sort of dream sent to lead her to the box in the dell. And that's true in a way. If it hadn't been for the ghost of Edmund Cope, she'd never have found the box.'

Sarah and the boys were sitting on the grass by the landing-stage. Miss Maybury had wanted to be alone with her letter and her poems.

'What I want to know,' said Tom, 'is how you came to be on the spot, Graham?'

Graham was sitting chewing a blade of grass, staring at the river.

'Just a hunch,' he said slowly. 'Well, perhaps a bit more than a hunch.' He was clearly feeling ashamed, but he told them the story.

When he'd arrived at the rowing club that morning the Skipper had been out on the river and he'd had to wait for him to come back. He'd watched him as he rowed in, admiring that strong, powerful, languid rowing action. Just for a moment he'd had the feeling that it brought something to mind though he couldn't think what.

He'd told the Skipper all about the strange happenings at Lockets and the Skipper had promised that he'd look into it. Graham had noticed, though, that he had seemed very anxious to make sure that the Clover Club definitely weren't going near Lockets today.

It was only afterwards that Graham had realised what was familiar about the rowing action. He'd had a sudden vivid mental picture of the ghost of Edmund Cope rowing out of sight round the bend in the river on the previous night. Suddenly he'd wondered if that were the reason the ghost had been able to outpace him so easily. It had seemed a crazy thought, but he was disturbed; uneasy. With nothing else to do, he had decided to drift over in the direction of Lockets and it was while he was wandering around in the woods that he had heard Sarah scream.

'I'm glad you did,' said Sarah. 'He'd have got away if it hadn't been for you.' He shot her a grateful glance.

'And look who's coming now,' said Tom.

A boat was coming into view from the Cherringham direction. Rowing it was Peter Warden. He was still wearing the blazer but he had removed the hat and wig. He pulled in beside the boathouse, out of view of the house, and stood up in the boat, holding on to the post. They all got up and went over to him.

'I'd like to know,' he said, 'what you're going to do – about me, I mean.' He looked very frightened and dishevelled, not at all the confident person Sarah had met in Hamblesey.

'I don't want to see you again,' said Graham, 'that's for sure. At the rowing club or anywhere else.'

'Are you going to tell the police?'

'We haven't decided yet,' said Tom.

'Before you go,' said Sarah, 'would you mind telling us a few things. Why you were searching the house, for example. And what gave you the idea you could get away with pretending to be Edmund Cope?'

'I was searching the house because I couldn't be sure the box hadn't been found,' he said. 'Maybe by Miss Maybury. Maybe by her parents. Then she overheard me, but instead of being frightened she started calling to me and it dawned upon me that she thought I was Edmund Cope come back to her.'

'So you thought you would encourage her. So that you'd be able to go and ask her to meet you in the secret place? It seemed a marvellous short cut to finding out where it was? You knew you wouldn't really have to go and meet her there. You could just follow her and find out where it was, then go back later.'

'Yes.'

'So you followed Sarah,' said Tom.

'Yes. Or rather, I followed you two first of all. It was a bit of a shock to find you kids at the house this morning because Graham had told me all about what was happening and that you wouldn't be coming back here till tomorrow. Still, at least you weren't there when I came and talked to Miss Maybury. I knew I could convince her with my disguise because she's pretty short-sighted.'

'Chump!' said Graham savagely to himself.

Peter Warden fingered the lapel of his blazer.

'You know, these aren't stage clothes,' he said, and there was pride in his voice. 'They *were* Edmund Cope's. I've collected everything I could of his.'

'Including the handkerchief you threw down to Miss Maybury?' said Sarah.

'Oh, yes, that was really his. I didn't like parting with it, but I was after bigger game.'

'But how did you manage to speak in his voice?' asked Rodge, with almost a grudging admiration. 'That's what really threw me.'

'I've got a recording of his voice,' said Peter Warden eagerly, 'the only one in existence. He's reading his poems. I've really worked hard copying it – for a long time, not just for this. You know, you really ought to join the Society and hear it sometime –'

He stopped.

'You think I've behaved badly, don't you,' he said, 'and I suppose I have. But I've loved Edmund Cope just as much as Miss Maybury ever has. You know the reason I took up rowing and became good at it? Because he did.'

'I think,' said Sarah, 'that you really loved dressing up as Edmund Cope and pretending to be him.'

His smile gleamed dazzlingly. For a moment he was Edmund Cope again.

'Perhaps you've hit the nail on the head, young lady,' he

said. He paused. 'Do you know how Edmund Cope died? He was called the Mad Major. There've been lots of people called that but he must have been one of the originals. He attacked a whole pack of German aeroplanes single-handed to hold them off from his aerodrome while his fellow-pilots got airborne. Went down in flames, riddled with bullets ...'

Sarah saw Graham's eyes open wide.

'... no wonder she's never forgotten him. He was the most perfect human being who ever lived. Brilliant mind, dazzling appearance, superb courage ...'

'It's a pity,' said Graham sourly, 'that you're not more like him. You only dress up like him.'

Peter Warden seemed to shrink again. He sat down in the boat.

'Just a minute,' said Sarah, 'there's something else. Last night when we chased you along the river, where did you disappear to after you tied your boat up at Willow Cottage?'

He turned and shrugged. 'I walked home. Just as I was going to row past the cottage it struck me as being a good idea to stop there. Make you believe I really was a ghost.'

'No wonder Graham couldn't catch you,' said Sarah. 'You – his rowing coach of all people.'

'We'll let you know what we decide,' said Tom curtly.

They watched him disappear round the bend in the river towards Hamblesey. They never saw him again. When Sarah passed his terraced cottage in Duckbury some weeks later, it was empty.

Miss Maybury wasn't by the dining room window when they left her that afternoon. She was in the sitting room with her letter and poems.

She accepted now that Edmund Cope was dead and would never come springing over the landing-stage and walking up the lawns to call for her again but she knew now also and for certain that he *had* loved her. They were one again and she was happy.

'We'll be back tomorrow,' Tom told her cheerfully, 'and this time we promise. We really will start to tidy up the house and grounds!'

'You won't be getting rid of the Clover Club for a long time yet,' said Rodge.

They were nice sentiments but surely there was something wrong with them, thought Sarah. However, she didn't comment. Instead she kissed Miss Maybury on the cheek. And Miss Maybury put her arms around Sarah's neck and pressed her cheek close to hers.

They cycled to the main road in silence and there halted to split up for the day. They were all starving. Graham sat astride his bike, staring ahead.

The Clover Club had its own problems, as Sarah had already remembered, the chief of them being that she was strictly speaking no longer a member.

'Actually,' said Graham, 'I've been thinking about that picture you gave me, Sarah. I was a bit hasty. It is authentic. I wouldn't like you to think I was being –'

'No – no,' she said hastily. 'I didn't think you were being – anything.'

'I was a fool to go and tell the Skipper, an absolute idiot. I was really taken in by him. I ought to be kicked out of the Clover Club for that.'

'Rodge and I were fooled by him as well,' said Tom solemnly, but Sarah saw that he and Rodge were winking at her behind Graham's back.

'You're all being nice to me,' said Graham gloomily.

He shifted uneasily in his saddle.

'If I'm still acceptable as a member myself,' he said, 'I wonder if I could propose that our present temporary member might be made a full member. It seems to me she's done more than enough to – to – if she wants to, that is . . .'

'Don't see any great problems about that,' said Tom weightily.

'Could go on the agenda tomorrow,' said Rodge, thrusting his hands into his pockets and swaying backwards and forwards while puffing his cheeks out, so that his bike almost fell over.

'Then Sarah,' said Graham, 'any chance of getting hold of a picture of Edmund Cope for me to put on the wall?'

He gave Sarah the most dazzling smile she had ever seen.

'So we don't even bother to come home for lunch these days?' said her mother, when she got in. 'Gillian's been ringing you. Wants to know what you've been doing with yourself?'

'Gillian!' Sarah wanted to laugh. Was it only last Thursday evening she'd been trying to get Gillian to accompany her to a spooky old house called Lockets where some batty old lady had lived?

Her world had changed since then, just as Miss Maybury's had. The excitement, romance and adventure she had found only in those photographs had come to life. And she had found the Clover Club.

Madford Rowing Club held their annual garden party at Lockets a few weeks later with Miss Maybury's permission. It was a heavenly place for it now that the Clover Club had done their tidying up, with help from senior members of the rowing club. It was also the occasion for the baptism of the new boat which Miss Maybury had insisted on buying for the rowing club. She was in danger of becoming their patron.

The boys took Sarah out in the boat and it was wonderful to be on the river in that still-hot summer. But Sarah was thinking, inevitably, of that other garden party, the garden party of the pictures. She wondered if Miss Maybury were, too.

Miss Maybury was seated beneath a parasol on the lawns, watching the activity around her, and dreaming. She looked happy. She was no longer wearing her 1914 dress. Sarah had prevailed upon her parents to take her into Cherringham and buy her a new one. It had been a memorable occasion from the moment they took her out to the car.

Lockets and Miss Maybury were slowly changing, slowly coming into the present day. In some ways, Sarah was sorry.

TARGET NON-FICTION

General Non-fiction
And biography

108906	Elizabeth Gundrey **THE SUMMER BOOK**	(illus)	45p
113594	Larry Kettelkamp **INVESTIGATING UFOs**	(illus)	50p
114396	Carey Miller **THE TARGET BOOK OF FATE & FORTUNE**	(illus)	50p
10823X	Christopher Reynolds **CREATURES OF THE BAY**	(illus)	50p
112369	David Shaw **CRAFTS FOR GIRLS**	(illus)	50p

Quiz And Games

102843	Nicola Davies **THE TARGET BOOK OF FUN AND GAMES**	(illus)	50p
10532X	**THE 2nd TARGET BOOK OF FUN AND GAMES**	(illus)	50p
109465	**THE 3rd TARGET BOOK OF FUN AND GAMES**	(illus)	50p
115198	**THE TARGET BOOK OF JOKES**		40p
116232	Harry Baron **THE TARGET BOOK OF MAGIC**	(illus)	70p
118340	G. J. B. Laverty **THE TARGET BOOK OF CROSSWORDS FOR FUN**		50p
117115	D. & C. Power **THE TARGET BOOK OF PICTURE PUZZLES**		40p
118855	Fred Reinfeld **THE TARGET BOOK OF CHESS**	(illus)	60p

TARGET STORY BOOKS

Fantasy And General Fiction

	Elisabeth Beresford		
101537	AWKWARD MAGIC	(illus)	60p
10479X	SEA-GREEN MAGIC	(illus)	60p
101618	TRAVELLING MAGIC	(illus)	60p
	Eileen Dunlop		
119142	ROBINSHEUGH	(illus)	60p
	Maria Gripe		
112288	THE GLASSBLOWER'S CHILDREN	(illus)	45p
	Joyce Nicholson		
117891	FREEDOM FOR PRISCILLA		70p
	Hilary Seton		
106989	THE HUMBLES	(illus)	50p
109112	THE NOEL STREATFEILD CHRISTMAS HOLIDAY BOOK	(illus)	60p
109031	THE NOEL STREATFEILD EASTER HOLIDAY BOOK	(illus)	60p
105249	THE NOEL STREATFEILD SUMMER HOLIDAY BOOK	(illus)	50p

Humour

	Eleanor Estes		
107519	THE WITCH FAMILY	(illus)	50p
	Felice Holman		
11762X	THE WITCH ON THE CORNER	(illus)	50p
	Spike Milligan		
105672	BADJELLY THE WITCH	(illus)	60p
109546	DIP THE PUPPY	(illus)	60p
	Christine Nostlinger		
107438	THE CUCUMBER KING	(illus)	45p
	Mary Rogers		
119223	A BILLION FOR BORIS		60p

0426 Film And TV Tie-ins

	Kathleen N. Daly		
200187	RAGGEDY ANN AND ANDY (Colour illus)		75p ◆*
	John Ryder Hall		
11826X	SINBAD AND THE EYE OF THE TIGER		70p* ◆
	John Lucarotti		
11535X	OPERATION PATCH		45p
	Pat Sandys		
119495	THE PAPER LADS		60p ◆
	Alison Thomas		
115511	BENJI		40p

†For sale in Britain and Ireland only.
*Not for sale in Canada.
◆ Film & T.V. tie-ins.

If you enjoyed this book and would like to have information sent to you about other TARGET titles, write to the address below.

You will also receive:
A FREE TARGET BADGE!
Based on the TARGET BOOKS symbol — see front cover of this book — this attractive three-colour badge, pinned to your blazer-lapel or jumper, will excite the interest and comment of all your friends!

and you will be further entitled to:
FREE ENTRY INTO THE TARGET DRAW!
All you have to do is cut off the coupon below, write on it your name and address in *block capitals,* and pin it to your letter. Twice a year, in June, and December, coupons will be drawn 'from the hat' and the winner will receive a complete year's set of TARGET books.

Write to:

TARGET BOOKS
44 Hill Street
London W1X 8LB

cut here

Full name ....

Address..

....

....

Age.....................

PLEASE ENCLOSE A SELF-ADDRESSED STAMPED ENVELOPE WITH YOUR COUPON!